CROSSED

STAR BREED: BOOK NINE

ELIN WYN

QUINN

"Almost got you, you weaselly little bastard," I muttered, fingers flying over the keyboard.

For two weeks I'd been chasing this little worm through security.

Slowly building a honeypot, nothing too obvious, just enough of a chink in the armor that would tempt someone looking for information on Orem Station.

On us.

From behind black ice walls of code I lurked, waiting for my prey to take the bait.

"Come on," I whispered, watching the screens surrounding me. "Just a little closer…"

"Quinn? Got a minute?" Ronan's voice snapped in my earpiece.

"Not really," I growled. "Is it important?"

"Maybe," he paused. "At least, Nixie thinks so."

I rolled my eyes.

"But this time, I think she might be right."

In the control room that had become Ronan's office, I found Hakon and Davien sprawled in the low chairs Nadira had somehow thought would be welcoming for visiting dignitaries. Not that many dignitaries were going to be comfortable visiting with us any time soon.

I winced when I saw Nixie. She'd gone for pink and purple flashing stripes for her holographic body today.

She could've been trying to shock us, she'd been acting like a teenager for weeks.

But it wasn't going to work, other than nearly blinding us.

We'd grown up with Doc, after all.

"I really think it's a match," she insisted, throwing up a screen on the wall behind her. "Just listen."

"I don't see how it could be," Davien cut her off.

"How should I know how?" she swung her feet from where she perched on Ronan's desk, deliberately not meeting his eyes. "But the voice print matches what's on file in the old Daedalus records."

My chest tightened, just a bit.

"I can't believe you even have those files," Hakon sighed.

"It's just taken me a while to go through everything." For the first time, the AI sounded and looked a bit embarrassed. "It's been pretty busy since we got here, and there was a lot of stuff, and it was hard to tell what was important because it was Doc's work and what was just her planning or dreaming-"

"More like scheming," I interrupted, face twisting into a wry grin.

"Tell me again what the message said," Ronan ordered, rubbing his eyes.

Somehow, no matter how helpful Nixie was being, it seemed inevitable you'd end up with a headache.

"I was bored with scanning for traffic in our region, and everything was boring in the hub, but then there was this little bounce off of a relay station not too far from the Areitis Sector. And that was interesting, because I didn't remember ever getting anything out of there before," she babbled.

Void save us from a bored AI.

"Nobody deals with the Areitis Sector," Davien said. "Too much trouble."

"But all of those interesting megacorps are there!" Nixie's black eyes sparkled. "Just imagine what they're hiding in their memory banks."

"They're hiding snakes' nests that don't pay if they can help it," I declared.

It was true, and like everything else we'd been dealing with, yet more fallout from the failed Empire.

Governance rights to the Areitis Sector had been

purchased by ThallaCorp from the Empire almost three hundred years ago.

I'm sure it made sense to them at the time. One less area to try to keep in line, and a quick influx of cash to pay the mercenaries the Empire needed to straighten out their little problems at home.

ThallaCorp wanted free rein for mining, industrial plants, whatever.

But in the time since, ThallaCorp had broken down, divided and fractured into dozens of ravenous competing corporations.

They were just as bad, if not worse, than the warlords of the Fringe.

They were businesses.

And all they cared about was the bottom line.

"We don't deal with Areitis, Nixie," I explained. "It's too complicated, even for us."

"Actually," Ronan sat back, staring at the ceiling, "Doc did send a team out. Years ago now."

"I don't have a list of the men who went," Nixie whispered. "But this message, I'm pretty sure it's a match to the voiceprint of one of your brothers."

"Let's hear it," I said. "We'll know for certain."

A hiss and crackles filled the air. "...contract failed... betrayed... extraction...Heladae..."

And then it faded away.

"Where's the rest of it?" Davien snapped.

Nixie threw her hands up. "That's all I could clean up out of the message. It's been bouncing around the nets for a long time, degrading the quality with every bounce." She threw a screen up on the wall facing her and an image filled it.

"I took a peek through some of the Imperial astrophysics lenses," she explained. "It's like someone put up a whole series of satellites around the inhabited systems in that sector. Kind of like a shield, or an alarm system maybe."

"Interesting, but not our problem," I said. "You can't tell me you got a print off of that sample."

"But I did!" The image changed, morphing into a series of scratchy lines, as she displayed the graph for the extracted bits of recording over another, unbroken line.

She played the message again, cleaned up, the hisses and pops gone.

"That almost sounds like Torik," I admitted grudgingly.

"No fair!" she pouted. "It took me hours and hours to go through all the recorded messages from the old Daedalus files. Well, maybe minutes. And you guessed it right away."

Ronan's expression was grim. "Did you find mission orders for Torik, or any of his squad?"

"Not yet," she chipped, "but I'm still looking. Can't

you just ask Doc if she remembers where Torik went, and who went with him?"

"No!" we answered in unison.

"Doc is…" Davien started, then caught himself.

"If it *is* Torik," I tried, "wouldn't it be nice if we brought him home as a surprise for her?"

And if it wasn't, or if the message was faulty, we couldn't be responsible for getting her hopes up.

"Maybe someone should go take a look," Ronan mused. "The Empire might decide the lease is up on that sector, and we might as well have some current intel."

"Sounds like he might have gotten into a bit of trouble," Hakon added.

"I hope not," Nixie muttered, biting her lip.

"What's wrong?" I asked, knowing I wasn't going to like the answer.

"The best I can piece together," she whispered, "your friend sent that message three years ago."

TRINI

It was a good thing the tips were plentiful, because I was going to need a new set of air boots by the time this shift ended.

"Over here, Trini!" Ondar, one of my regulars, called out.

"Right there," I smiled, hoping he wouldn't see past the plastic grin I'd had plastered to my face for the last hour.

Just because it was still morning didn't mean a thing. Not here.

The low pulsing music throbbed in time with the flickering lights. The stage in the middle of the room was draped with rhythmic shadows.

Pausing to dodge around another drunk, I slapped absently at a hand that stole across my hip.

"Oh, come on, honey. Why don't you take a seat and watch the show with me?"

"You know perfectly well that's against the rules, Girdar," I ground out. "Why don't I freshen up that drink for you."

"Sure, sure." But his eyes were fixed on Risti as she twisted and bent around the dancing poles, the spangled scraps of fabric catching the light.

Making my way through the crowded floor, I leaned against the bar.

"We need to start charging more," I groused.

"What's this *we*, little girl?" Russar snapped back, but by the broad grin, I knew the burly bar owner hadn't lost his temper with his patrons yet.

He wouldn't, not as long as they kept ordering his high-end stock.

And while their eyes were on Risti's gyrations, they seldom noticed if it was a little watered down.

"I know, I know. I only work here. But as your senior employee, I think that should give me a little bit of say in how we run this place."

He handed me a glass filled with light, sparkling trakko, and patted my hand in commiseration.

"I know it's wild when your friend is dancing, but you've got to admit," he waved at the crowded room, "she packs them in."

It was true.

Risti didn't technically work at the Merry Storm-cloud. She considered her occasional early afternoon sets here as advertising for her real job, over at Momma Deese's pleasure house.

It was a good thing all around.

We won, because all the men wanted to come and see her.

She won, because a good portion of them would come back and set up appointments at Deese's for later.

And that's how things worked here in Rondi, the pleasure capital of Heladae.

Everybody made a deal, everybody tried to get ahead.

It was just good business.

And in a sector run by the megacorps, you couldn't get away from it.

Russar filled the orders I'd sent ahead from my tablet, but instead of placing them on my tray, he set them aside.

"I'll have one of the other runners take them out." He shook his head at my sour expression. "I'll make sure you get your split."

"If I'm gonna put up with people's hands on my ass, I better be getting my split," I muttered, knowing he couldn't hear me over the music.

Probably.

"Why don't you take this one over to table eleven?"

He set a tall glass on the center of my tray. "Special request."

My eyes narrowed. "That's never a good thing," I said, waiting for an explanation.

Russar sighed dramatically. "It's just Makkar. He asked if he could see you for a few minutes."

I didn't bother to hide my rolling eyes.

"We haven't dated for what, two, three years? I don't think he gets special favors."

For all that Russar was willing to work himself and anyone else into the ground to keep his bar running, none of that work ethic had rubbed off on his younger brother.

Makkar could be fun to hang out with, sure. But after a while, I got tired of babysitting someone with a lot of big talk he wasn't willing to work for.

"You just want me to work for free in the family business. But we're not getting back together," I insisted, picking up the drink for table eleven. "I'm more likely to go out with you than him, any day."

Russar laughed. Easy for him. He and his husband had been partnered up longer than anyone I knew.

As I headed away from the bar, I ran through my mantra.

Focus on the good things, Trini. You've got a solid job, a place of your own, friends, and good money coming in. You don't need anything else.

At least table eleven was farther away from the noise and strobing lights of Risti's performance.

That surely counted as another good thing.

"Hey, baby!" Makkar slid out of his chair, lunging forward to hug me before I could dance away.

"Ow!" A sharp pain caught at my shoulder and I stepped back.

"Sorry, baby," Makkar took the tray from me, pulled another chair out from the table. "I think I've got a pin or something in my coat. Keep meaning to look for it, but you know how it is."

Yup. I knew exactly how it was.

"Print," I ordered, holding my datapad out for his thumb.

"Why you gotta be so harsh?" Makkar whined as he approved the order. With a stingy tip.

"Not harsh, just busy. Look around, we're slammed here."

"Not so busy you can't sit down, right?" His trademark charming grin flashed, right on schedule.

And... sure, we were busy. But my boss had pretty much ordered me over here.

And my feet were screaming for a break.

"Fine. Five minutes," I said as I dropped into the chair.

A thought struck me as I took a deep breath. "Aren't you hooked up with Mada these days? She seems like someone who should be able to keep you busy enough that you don't have time to hang around here, bothering folks."

"Man, Trini," he groaned, shaking his head. "That is one stone cold bitch." He waggled his eyebrows like an eight-year-old. "But she can make it worth it."

"Don't tell me anything further," I snapped.

I really didn't want to know any details. One, because that was gross.

And two, because Mada Sommu would probably be happy for her boytoy to call her a stone cold bitch.

And in no way, shape, or form did I want to get tangled up in her business.

"Trini!" a voice shouted from the darkness. "Where's that drink?"

"Break time's over," I pushed back from the table. "Try not to get into any trouble, would you? Your brother's a good guy."

"Be seeing you," he smirked.

Not if I could help it.

QUINN

"New here, honey?" The golden skinned brunette slid towards me from the doorway, somehow managing to drape herself on the edge of the half-wall in a manner that wasn't just suggestive, it was downright declamatory.

"Just passing through, looking for a friend," I answered, shifting my small bag higher on my shoulder.

"Oh. I can be real friendly," she purred, stretching to display her curves, her long dark braids cascading down her back.

I shook my head, amused, if not aroused. "I have no doubts about that." I paused, thinking. "I expect you see a fair number of visitors to Rondi as they pass through, correct?"

"Honey, everyone comes down the Boulevard

when they first arrive. They wouldn't miss the view for the world." She adjusted the neckline of her catsuit.

"My friend, he looks a little bit like me, same general height and build, darker hair."

At least it had been the last time I remembered seeing Torik.

"Oh no, honey," she ran her fingertips down one shoulder, curved herself around my back to emerge on my other side. "I'd remember if I saw someone as fine as you recently."

"It might've been a little further back than recently," I admitted. "More like two or three years ago."

She stepped back and laughed, honest amusement ringing clear in her voice. "Honey, you don't imagine anybody remembers anything from two years ago around here, do you?" She shook her head, the silvery bells braided into her hair tinkling with every movement. "Remembering is not what people come to Rondi for."

I slipped her a credit chip, more than enough to make up for her time, and continued my way down the crowded street.

I'd been sent on missions to some of the wilder areas of the Fringe, and the Under of Orem Station was certainly no chaste playground.

But the city of Rondi, the only large population

center on the entire planet, appeared to be dedicated to pleasure.

It made a sort of sense. In a sector devoted to business, there had to be somewhere devoted to play.

And they took it very, very seriously.

Streets upon streets were filled with stores, beautiful holographic forms modeling high-end fashion and scanty sleepwear, next to tiny shops filled with exquisite art. Musicians and magicians performed on every corner.

Barkers stood outside gambling halls and arcades, coaxing passersby to try their luck.

And the more carnal forms of pleasure were on full, unabashed display, as well.

Restaurants from which enticing odors wafted were sandwiched between storefronts promising the ultimate in relaxation or unheard-of titillation.

And by the position of the bright suns overhead, it would be a few hours yet until night fell and the serious games started.

Well, if Torik had to be stranded somewhere, he probably could've chosen a worse place to spend a few years.

I stepped into yet another bar, pausing in the doorway to let my eyes adjust to the low light, glancing over the darkened room.

The space was long and narrow, with a small

rectangular stage taking up the center of the front half of the bar.

A young woman gyrated on the stage to a low thumping beat, her every movement the focus of a crowd of surprisingly well-behaved admirers.

Three runners brought drinks out and took orders on small commtabs.

Nothing but another bar.

Nothing here I needed to investigate further.

As I was turning to leave, another young woman hustled by with a tray, calling over her shoulder as she passed, "Haven't seen you for a while! I'll get your regular order started."

That was interesting. And worth staying for.

"I appreciate it, Miss, but I don't think I have a regular order. I just got on-planet."

She spun towards me, hazel eyes wide, short curly hair flying around her face.

"Oh, I'm so sorry!" she exclaimed. "Standing there in the doorway, I would have sworn you were someone else. He hasn't been in for a while. Can't imagine what I was thinking."

I glanced around the room again. It stretched back, broken into sections that grew ever darker.

"If you can find me a seat away from the music," I waved at the stage, "why don't I see what my regular would've been?"

She smiled and shook her head. "I'm not sure if you want to do that. It's not exactly our most popular drink. Most people find it pretty bitter."

I swung my bag off my shoulder and stretched a bit. "That's alright. I'm not big on most sweets. It runs in the family."

She gave an exaggerated shudder. "Alright then, but I warned you."

She started to lead me to a table to the side of the stage, but I stepped back.

"Any chance of finding a quieter corner?"

Her head tilted, eyes narrowed and appraising. "Are you sure? Most of our guests appreciate the show."

I glanced again at the woman dancing.

Certainly attractive enough, and obviously very limber.

But not particularly interesting. Not nearly as fascinating as the woman standing before me.

"That's alright. I'm not big on loud noises, or crowds, really."

She nodded. "We do have a quieter section; it's almost empty right now. Would that do?"

"Sounds perfect."

She brushed my upper arm to guide me back, and I stiffened.

Her touch, her scent, lit a slow fuse in the back of

my brain. Something deep in my blood stirred, hungry and possessive.

Apparently being in a city full of raging pheromones was having an effect on me after all.

Quickly I shook it off and followed her into the depths of the building. We passed a long bar, it's U shape jutting into the room, dividing the front, louder section from the back.

A large, burly bald man watched me carefully as I followed my hostess.

"Is your bartender always so friendly?" I asked.

"Russar? He's the owner, so he takes a reasonable interest in everyone new who comes in." She glanced back over her shoulder at me and raked her eyes over my body. "Especially ones that look like they could do some damage to the place."

I guess I couldn't argue with that.

"But he's a sweetie, really. He must've just been trying to figure out if he'd seen you before, same as me."

Sure.

"Nope, first time to town, first time on the planet at all."

"I don't have to ask if you're going to have a good time." She pulled out a chair at a table off to the side of the back room, her smile easy. "Everyone does here. That's the point."

"I've noticed that," I agreed.

"I'll be right back with your drink."

She walked away and I watched her get into a short exchange with the man behind the bar. One hand on her hip, I didn't have to have enhanced hearing to know she wasn't putting up with his concerns.

"You always say customers are our guests, until they screw up. He hasn't done anything for you to be in such a fuss over," she insisted.

"Yet," he grumbled, but poured the drink anyway.

Russar might be the owner, but he seemed to take his staff's opinions into some account. Still, I didn't think he was a sweetheart, no matter what she said.

This section was mostly empty, the majority of the bar's patrons choosing to watch the show.

The only other occupied table held a young man with brown hair in what was probably meant to be artful disarray, but to my eye, it looked sloppy. He slouched in his chair, a stained tan coat half on the floor.

He nursed a drink, eyes fixed on my curly-haired waitress.

And while she was charming, something about his expression bothered me.

As if he was waiting for something, expectant.

Pull it together, Quinn, and get down to business. Whatever his game was, he wasn't my target.

She came back with my drink, a short wide glass filled halfway with a dark brown liquid.

"If you hate it, I'll get you something else," she promised.

I tasted it warily.

Took another sip. Then another.

Her eyes widened and her fingers danced at her throat.

"Or I'll just bring you another one of those," she said.

"No need, but I wanted to ask you—"

A shout from the bar cut me off.

"Trini!"

She rolled her eyes. "I'll be back in a second, hold on."

I took another sip from the glass, letting the sharp taste roll over my tongue.

It wasn't bad, different, couldn't quite place it.

But I could imagine Torik drinking something like this.

After some heated discussion at the bar, Trini stomped off to the front of the room.

A moment later, Russar headed my way until he stopped, looming over the table.

"What outfit are you with?" he barked out. "None of the corps use my place for recruiting, and you're not wearing anyone's badge."

"I'm not with any of the corps," I said evenly. "Not looking to join up, either. Not looking for a hard time, not looking to cause trouble. Just passing through."

"That's what they all say," he muttered.

"Really, I'm looking for an old friend who I heard was in the neighborhood, and maybe a room for the night."

"I don't know anything about a friend of yours," he finally said. He paused again, doing some sort of silent evaluation. "But Trini likes you. She doesn't like most people. We've got a room. Nothing fancy, and the elevator doesn't work half the time."

"My legs carry me just fine," I said. "I can use the stairs."

I reached toward my pocket for a credit chip, stopping at his narrowed eyes.

"Easy there," he rumbled.

"Just trying to settle my bill, since I didn't have a chance to with Trini," I said, nodding towards my drink. "And figured you'd want the room paid for upfront."

Bushy eyebrows came together as he frowned. "You can thumb for it, the same as everything else."

As Trini had led me to the back of the room, I'd noticed the other waitresses holding commtabs towards the patrons. I'd thought it was just for ordering, but now it clicked.

Our research on the Areitis Sector had been rushed, and apparently at least one thing had slipped through. Hopefully nothing else vital had.

"Afraid I can't. My thumbprint won't be connected to any bank account here," I explained.

"Everyone has an account linked to their print," he insisted.

"We can try if you like." A thought struck me. "Maybe if it comes up zero, you'll know I'm not actually registered with one of the corps. If I was, they'd want to be able to pay me, right?"

"Maybe," he said, torn between wanting to get paid, and still wanting to toss me out.

I couldn't blame him.

"Look, run the chip first, then you'll know you're covered either way," I offered. "We'll make it into a bet. If an account shows up for me, I'll leave, and you can keep the money."

Now to hope that Nixie hadn't decided to be 'helpful'.

Russar slipped the chip into a small opening in the side of the commtab and frowned again.

"Credits are good, but this isn't a local encryption."

I nodded. "Like I said, I'm not from around here."

He nodded. "Alright, now pay for it like normal."

After a moment's hesitation, I pressed my thumb to the square black surface set into the front of the tablet.

As long as it was just a 'print reader, I'd be fine. If it was a DNA reader, well, a lot of people got a little enhanced these days. But it seemed unlikely they'd have something quite that sophisticated on every server's tablet.

The icons spun. And spun. And spun some more.

And finally stopped, flashing a warning. *No entry found. Please seek alternate payment.*

Russar scowled at the device, then shrugged. "Strange, but not unheard of, I suppose. When you finish that," he nodded to the drink, "come up to the bar and I'll have the card ready for your room." He turned to walk away, then stopped. "You said you're not looking for trouble. Whatever you're looking for, keep it out of my place."

By the time I finished my drink, Trini still hadn't returned, but her admirer had finally left, slipping out a side door.

For what it was worth, I was glad that Russar seemed to keep such a tight eye on the place. He didn't seem the sort that would let one of his staff get hassled.

As he'd warned me, the elevator was broken. Three easy flights up found me in the room.

It was basic enough. A layered foam bed pulled out from the wall, a short dresser for clothing, a simple cleaning and drying tube.

Good.

Basic made it easier to scan for bugs.

Satisfied I was truly alone, I unpacked quickly, setting up a secure channel for the comm cube.

"Reporting in," I spoke softly. The room might be clean of bugs, but no telling yet how thin the walls were.

"No sign of Torik yet, but I have a possible lead."

"A possible possibility?" Mack scoffed, his voice tinny over the line. "Doesn't sound like much."

"Yeah, but it's what we've got. I'll see what I can do about making it a little stronger. Nixie still pouting?"

I'm not pouting. I'm angry with you, she chirped. *You could've taken one of my extensions with you just as easily as the comm cube.*

"Nope," I answered her. "You haven't learned much about discretion yet. And there's a whole world of new servers for you to want to play in."

I have so learned discretion! she squealed. *I haven't told anyone about things in other people's medical records for weeks and weeks!*

"Nixie, if Granny Z wanted a surprise party, she would have told someone about her birthday herself," I explained.

Again.

Through the silence came a soft sniffle, and I rolled my eyes. Someone was going to have to find a way to control our little AI's appetite for teledramas.

"Nixie, if you're good, I'll make sure to bring some files home for you, alright?" I finally conceded.

Encrypted ones? came the soft reply.

"The hardest codes I can find, I promise."

I clicked off, tapped one finger against the cube, and tucked it away, still thinking.

It would have been useful to bring Nixie, but she was just too reckless, possibly bringing attention to the mission when we didn't want it.

She was our ace in the hole, and unless absolutely necessary, I didn't want the megacorps to know she existed.

There was something here, a trail just waiting to be uncovered.

I could feel it.

And somehow the woman, Trini, was the key.

TRINI

"Do not tell me Makkar is here to try to get back together with you," Risti insisted from her perch in the changing room.

It wasn't much of a dressing room really, just a section cut out of the back storeroom, thin sheets of permasteel roughly welded together to make the walls, a drape over the door.

Considering how much extra business Risti brought in every time she performed, I always thought we should make something nicer.

Maybe even with real furniture.

But she insisted she didn't care.

"Getting ready, I'm not looking at the room, I'm thinking about the act," she had explained once. "And after, I just want to be done and take a nap." Her teeth gleamed white against the dark green lipstick she wore. "By myself or with some new friends. It depends how it all goes, you know?"

So here we were, perched on crates that at least were softened by cushions covered with a deep burgundy brocade I'd found in one of the smaller shops a few blocks off the Boulevard.

Her cleansers and creams lay strewn across a makeshift shelf topped by a broad mirror.

"No, he's not trying to get back together with me." I sighed, flopping back against the wall, trying to get comfortable. My shoulder was still sore from that stupid pin in Makkar's coat. "That was years ago, anyway. It's not like I was his one great love, that's for sure."

I picked up one of Risti's shimmering creams, held it against my skin.

"Wrong shade for you, love," she said, glancing over. "But you know I'd be happy to glam you up, anytime."

"Not happening," I told her. "It looks great on you, but I don't think I could carry all of it off," I explained, waving at the box of enhancements.

"Sure you could. Just, not for that jerk, alright? I mean, he's sorta cute, I'll give Makkar that," she said wiping away her eye makeup. "But if you want cute, it'd be easier to go to one of the gene splicers and custom order up a pet."

I covered my eyes with my hands.

As much as I hated to admit it, she kind of had a point. Charming, clumsy, and a little bit helpless, yeah, a baby zuhair might be pretty close.

"At least he came potty trained," I defended myself.

"Ewwww…" Risti flicked a hand. "Your problem is that you're too nice. But enough about that. Tell me about tall, dark, and yummy."

"Who?" I blinked.

She looked at me in the mirror and rolled her eyes. "Seriously? The delicious dish you walked into the back, who didn't even take a second glance at me because he was far too interested in watching you?"

"That's unlikely," I protested, picking up a tube of eye shimmer, which she promptly switched for another.

"Try that one, and keep talking."

I shook my head, then tried out the color. No, too bright, too attention grabbing. I grabbed a wipe to tone it down. "No idea. Russar wasn't sure about him, but that's nothing new. This guy doesn't exactly act like one of the corps mercs, but there's something odd about him." I checked the mirror again. Better. "He seems all right to me, honestly."

"I hope so, given the way he was checking you out," Risti teased, cleaning off a glittering layer of silver from her legs.

"I think you're imagining things," I said, handing her back the tube as she started to pack up her kit.

"I have eyes," Risti said. "And I am perfectly aware when I am being checked out and when I'm not. He wasn't paying attention to me, I promise you that." She stood and tossed her hair back into a messy bun. "If I'm gonna get a nap before work tonight, I better head out."

Risti hip-bumped me on her way through the narrow room. "And I want to hear all about your mysterious stranger just as soon as he makes contact."

I laughed, following her out into the back of the bar. "You're gonna be waiting a long time, girl."

But there he was, waiting at the table where I'd left him.

Risti flounced through on the way to the street, and he didn't even turn to watch her go.

I stayed for a moment in the shadow of the door, studying him.

I couldn't tell exactly why I thought I'd recognized him earlier.

He wasn't my irregular regular.

I snorted to myself.

Knock it off, Trini.

There're probably dozens of mercs out there who look like that. Bodywork and enhancers to look a little wild, a little scary.

That's all it was.

But I knew, even as I grabbed my commpad and headed to his table, that there was something more.

"Sorry about that. Russar needed some help in the front, then it was time for my break."

That wasn't exactly it, of course. Russar hadn't wanted me near the stranger until he had a chance to interrogate him.

And surprisingly enough, the stranger was still here, but without his bag, I noticed.

"Did he actually rent you a room?" I asked.

"Yeah," he grinned and his grim face suddenly turned charming. "We finally saw eye to eye on a few things."

Interesting.

"How long are you going to be staying here?" I wondered.

"Not sure," he admitted. "I'm trying to get a sense of the city, see if it makes sense for me to stay here or keep moving." He looked up, tilted his head to the side. "You wouldn't happen to know where I could find a reputable guide, do you? There're these everywhere," he gestured at the disk on the table, that popped up with advertisements for all the touristy things to do in the city. "But I'd like to get a sense of what the city is really like."

An utterly ridiculous thought swept through me.

"Well, I could find someone to cover a few hours for me..."

He smiled. "I'm in no hurry. I can wait." He held up the short glass.

I shuddered extravagantly. "First stop on your guided tour is for something that actually tastes good."

"I'll be here," he promised.

I stepped away, then turned back. "I don't even know your name. Or is that part of the mystique?"

The corners of his eyes crinkled just a bit. "There's no mystique at all, I promise. Just plain, regular Quinn."

I went to work the front of the house, emptier now that Risti's performance was over, but still full enough to keep me and the other servers busy.

When I ran back to the bar with my tray, Russar was frowning again.

"You can't be that worried if you let him have a room here," I said.

"His money is good," Russar admitted. "But he's not from around here."

"Nobody's from Rondi," I laughed. "Almost nobody, anyway."

"I don't mean just the city," Russar said. "Or even Heladae. I don't think he's from anywhere in the sector."

I stopped, blinking. "Well, that's..." I trailed off.

Not impossible, there was *some* trade between the

corps and the broken Empire out there, or what was left of it.

"I've never met anybody from outside the sector," I mused.

"Doesn't make him anything special," Russar growled. "Just different."

I could agree that Quinn was different, at least.

"So, you know how you've been saying I should take some time off?"

Black brows drew together. "I'm pretty sure I never said any such thing."

"But you would've if you'd thought of it," I pressed on.

"I haven't thought of it. Which is why I hadn't said anything like it."

"But if you had thought of it, you'd have said it, and I really appreciate it," I rushed. "I'm taking the evening off. I've already checked with the other girls, they'll be happy to take up the time."

Russar blinked, then narrowed his eyes. "What are you gonna do instead? You always want all the hours you can get."

"I'm gonna go play tour guide."

His look of shock was enough to make the rest of my shift fly by.

Finally free, I walked back to Quinn's table, where he was still nursing his drink.

"Out the door and half a block to the left is a shop with a bright pink door." I paused, waited for his nod. "Meet me there in twenty minutes."

He took another sip from the glass. "I think I can handle that."

I dashed up to my room, stripping off my working clothes almost as I went, tossed my clothes on the bed, and jumped into the cleaning tube.

By the time I was dry, five minutes were gone.

"Let's see what we can do."

Luckily there wasn't much clutter to distract me. A vase on the bedside table was filled with artificial flowers, gold and purple blossoms looming over a tacky statuette of a zuhair I'd won during a wild night out with Risti three months ago.

What could I say? We're easily amused.

Rifling through my closet, I pulled on a loose and breezy jade-colored dress embroidered with tiny white flowers at the hem that floated around my knees.

I glared at the tubes scattered across the dresser top.

Risti would know what to do with them. Risti wouldn't be intimidated by all that potential for ending up looking like a clown.

A tiny bit of gold shimmer and that was enough. Or at least as much as I was willing to experiment with.

I slipped into sandals and ran down the stairs, out the side door, and onto the Boulevard.

Why was I so excited? Was it just the adventure that came from being near a stranger, who, if Russar was right, someone that didn't even work for any of the corps?

No, there was plenty of excitement working at the Merry Stormcloud, plenty just living in a city like Rondi.

I didn't need to go looking for adventure.

There was something about him. Something that drew me, pulled me in.

Darting through the crowd of people, I craned my head to see him.

With that height, he'd be easy to spot.

But my stomach sank.

He wasn't here.

QUINN

G rumbling, I pushed my way back to the assigned meeting place.

A knot of people had formed, surging down the Boulevard in a tight cluster.

At the time, it had seemed the smart thing to do, flow with the stream, circle back to the shop with the pink door.

Now I was late, and irritated. I should have stayed put, made the crowd go around me.

But as soon as Trini stepped out from the bar, that all faded.

She stood in the street, searching back and forth through the throng, the fading evening suns picking out strands of gold and red in the waves of her tousled brown hair.

The light behind her picked out the vaguest shape of her body through a loose green dress that didn't cling to her, wasn't low-cut, wasn't revealing at all.

And still, something about it made my pulse run a little fast.

"Over here," I waved and a smile lit her face.

"I thought you hadn't waited!" she exclaimed

"Where would I go without my guide? Alright, where to first?"

"This is our first stop," she explained, grabbing my arm and tugging me after her.

"We're starting the day with cones," she exclaimed.

"With what?"

"Come on, anybody who can drink that stuff can't be afraid of a little cone." She tilted her head thoughtfully. "Are you allergic to anything?"

"I don't think so," I answered, somewhat confused. It would have been an odd oversight for Doc to make, but possible, maybe. "Nothing's ever come up."

"Well then, let's go in!"

We walked through the bright pink door into a room decorated in purple and orange, a cool white marble floor softly reflecting the colors. A light chill permeated the storefront, unfamiliar smells everywhere.

Trini bounced to the counter. "There's not even a line. That's a great sign."

"Haven't seen you in a while, kiddo," the woman behind the counter welcomed us, fine lines creasing her face, highlighting her smile.

"It's been a little busy," Trini said with a small shrug.

"Don't let that old slave driver keep you past your shift so much," the older woman scolded. "You let him take advantage of you."

"I like working for him, and I don't mind the overtime," Trini answered. "You never know when a little extra padding on the account is going to come in handy."

"That's true," the woman agreed. "Glad you decided to cut loose for a bit, though. What'll it be?"

"I'll have a chocolate almond mocha mint bomb." Trini's smile got broader with every word.

The woman grabbed a thin hollow golden cone and began scooping globs of something into it from small vats below the counter.

"Don't forget the sprinkles," Trini said.

"I'd never do that to you," the woman handed the towering thing to Trini. Now the globs had tiny multicolored flecks all over them.

It looked horribly, horribly wrong.

"What can I get for your friend?"

My mind stuttered. "I don't really think this is something I can eat."

"Nonsense," Trini insisted. "Cones are good. I'm sure they're probably good *for* you, too."

That seemed unlikely, but it was just as unlikely that I was going to get out of here without ordering something.

"What do you have that's plain?" I asked the woman behind the counter. "And small?"

The woman laughed. "She'll never admit it, but we do a pretty good vanilla."

"No. He's not having vanilla," Trini insisted. "He's here to have fun. He should have something like this."

"How about he has one of your flavors," the older woman argued on my behalf. "It might take a while to work up to all of them together."

"Fine," Trini sighed. "But don't forget he wants sprinkles, too."

I started to argue, but then she turned those huge eyes on me.

"Right. Sprinkles."

But there was only so far I was willing to go. When Trini reached toward the black square set into the countertop, I gently grabbed her wrist before she could press her thumbprint to it.

"Do you have the ability to take a chip?" I asked the store owner.

"I can handle that," she said. "Good manners are

always appreciated." She finished the transaction and winked at Trini. "Keep an eye on this one."

We headed out of the shop and the Boulevard was even busier than before.

"Let's go this way, it will be less crowded," Trini said, then, with a quick swipe of her pink tongue, took a lick of her treat.

I followed her, and soon enough the crowd emptied out, and I could hear the crashing of the sea.

"So you don't have anything linked to your print, at all?" Trini asked. "Isn't that inconvenient?"

"It hasn't been so far," I answered. "Don't you worry that it makes it far too easy to track everything you do?"

Trini took another lick of her cone and my throat tightened.

"Don't just stand there," she scolded. "It's going to melt all over your fingers."

She was right. I'd been so caught up watching her eat her cone, I hadn't even noticed the sticky drips down my hand.

I took a tentative bite. It was cold against my teeth, and far, far too sweet.

"It's, it's interesting." I managed.

"Cones aren't interesting," she laughed. "Cones are fantastic."

"I'm not sure what I think about the sprinkles."

"I will win that argument, I promise you," she said.

It was almost worth arguing, just to see the flash in her eyes, but I wanted information more. For now.

"So, everyone here has their thumbprint on file and access to all their information is linked? And you're ok with that?"

"Sure," she said, heading closer to the sounds of the ocean, salt air replacing the perfumed aroma of the Boulevard.

"Everyone works for the corps, one way or another. Even me," she continued.

She stopped as the street dead-ended, leaned against a waist- high wall that separated the street from the stretch of sand beyond.

"I mean, not directly. But the Merry Stormcloud, just like any of the businesses in Rondi, has to do their banking through Mada Sommu's corp. Price of business."

"And since the bar pays you, it goes through the corp accounts," I finished. "Every other business here is all linked together."

"It's not just here, it's how it is all through the sector," she explained, watching me as if I should know this. "It's just more efficient that way."

That was one way to describe it.

It was a remarkably efficient way to track everyone who participated in the economy. Not just their spending habits, but their movements, their routines.

I tapped my fingers on the wall, watching the waves crash against the wet sand.

Since Rondi was a tourist destination, shops here were more likely to be able to take alternate methods of payment.

But even here, the initial assumption was that you'd have a corporate account.

It seemed likely that the deeper you got into the sector, the more you'd almost *have* to have one, just to survive.

That was disturbing.

But there were always ways around surveillance.

No matter the trade off in convenience, there would always be a few who refused to play by the rules.

And chances were good that's where I'd find Torik.

Trini finished her cone and I offered her mine. "Don't you like it," she asked, her expression crestfallen.

"I do," I said hurriedly. "It's just a little too sweet for me."

She shook her head sadly but took it. "Not many things are considered a sin here," she said as she turned back to the wall. "But wasting a good cone would be."

Trini rested her elbows on the top of the wall as she licked the cone. I glanced at her, then quickly away, out to the wine-dark sea, tall-sailed boats cutting across the waves and back again, out for evening cruises.

A group of young boys played some sort of game

down the block under a flickering light, their shouts competing with the screeching of glossy black birds high above, cutting through the air.

"I love coming out here to watch the waves," she said softly. "When the storms come, they crash almost over the wall in places. It's so wild. Anything could happen."

I shuddered slightly, thinking about what Geir had said lived under the waters surrounding the compound where he'd freed Valrea. "Anything could, you're right."

In three quick bites of her white teeth, she crunched through the crispy golden cone, then boosted herself up, scrambling to the top of the wall.

"What are you doing?" I asked, startled.

"Feeling the wind," she answered, standing with her arms spread wide.

I shook my head, uneasy. While the wall was only waist high on the city side, the beach side was four or five yards below, piles of jagged rocks lying against the base.

Further down the walkway, I saw an opening cut through the wall, steps zigzagging down to the ocean.

"If you want to go to the beach, why don't we just take the stairs?"

It was a perfectly reasonable question, I thought, but she looked confused.

"I don't want to go to the beach," she said. "I just want to feel the wind for a bit."

The top of the wall was as broad as my hand, I told myself. It'd be fine.

"So," she said, walking a bit ahead of me. "Tell me about this person you're looking for. Lots of people come through the town. Maybe I've seen him, or at least heard of him."

I stepped quickly to keep by her side. "I think possibly you have," I agreed. "But first, tell me more about the person you thought I was when I came in this morning."

The wall had risen gradually as we talked, and her feet were now level with my shoulders. She didn't falter once, and I began to relax.

"That," she sighed. "I'm so sorry, I don't know why that happened. You guys don't look anything alike. Different color hair, different color skin, there's just something about where you were in the doorway."

"Tell me about him anyway," I said. "Now I'm curious."

"Fine, he's a trapper from up north, only comes into town every few months. His name is-"

A shout from the street distracted her and Trini turned, whipping her head towards the noise.

Without thinking, I reached up, batted the small ball out of the air, away from her.

But it didn't matter.

Trini flinched from the oncoming projectile, and stumbled backwards, losing her footing.

There was only a moment to see her pale frightened face before she fell, not even a scream, just a gasp.

With a quick leap, I jumped to the top of the wall, one arm hooked around the top, the other snagging her from the air before she fell onto the rocky beach below.

Before she could gasp again, we were back safely on the walkway, her soft form cradled in my arms.

A group of young boys ran up, eyes wide. "We're sorry, Jan threw wide, and I missed the hit, and then -"

"Be more careful," I growled, holding Trini's shaking body tightly against me. "And leave."

They left, quickly.

I leaned with my back against the wall, still holding her, waiting for my own heartbeat to settle.

Her shaking had stopped, the scent of her fear subsiding.

I swallowed hard, and again.

Knowing she'd been afraid, that they'd been the cause of it, it'd been all I could do not to tear into those boys.

Trini took a deep breath, then another. She squirmed, and reflexively I tightened my grip.

"Thank you. You can let me down now," she said in a small voice.

"Are you hurt?"

A long pause.

"No, just a little startled."

A different scent flooded the air and I stiffened.

Against every instinct I had, I set her down carefully.

She looked up at me, cheeks flushed, lips parted. "Thank you, again."

Then that irrepressible smile broke through. "Come on, let's go have some more fun!"

Mind whirling, I followed her as she tugged my hand, leading me back into the lights of the city.

Staring at her tiny fingers wrapped around my wrist, I shook my head.

I could break her grip in an instant.

Find another, more reliable source of information.

But really, I couldn't.

Just the scent of her, the touch of her, the feel of her in my arms.

And I didn't have any other choice.

TRINI

As I led Quinn through the streets, I fought to get my thoughts in order.

What on earth was I thinking?

I was still shaken, but not from my fall.

Maybe I should be, but something else had pushed that danger from my mind.

I could still feel his hard muscles under my hand from when he had clutched me to his chest.

He'd caught me so easily, so fast.

Who could move like that? Lift me so easily?

I wasn't a tiny slip of a thing, but in his arms, I'd felt like it.

And that wasn't all you felt, I chided myself.

Something about this man drew me in, made me want to learn more about him.

And I remembered Russar's warning.

Quinn was a stranger, a visitor. Not just in town for a vacation, but someone not even from the sector.

Whatever it was that I'd felt in his arms, it couldn't last.

But that didn't mean we couldn't have a nice evening out, right?

"Where are we going?" he asked as I tugged him along.

I smiled a little, relieved that his voice sounded so much calmer. For a terrible moment, I'd thought he was going to attack those kids back there.

Sure, they were careless, and sure, it could have gone wrong, but it was just as much my fault for being in a dangerous spot.

"Have I steered you wrong yet?" I called back over my shoulder. "And don't tell me about not liking the cones. Cones are fantastic, I think you'll just have to have a few more to work up your tolerance for sweetness."

"Wait, what?"

He'd have to wait, because I could hear the noise, feel the electricity in the air from where we were heading.

The street narrowed to an archway, covered with a shimmer of blue light.

There was just a moment of resistance as we stepped through.

Then we entered the world of the Carnival.

The Boulevard might be Rondi City's home for all pursuits in the sensual world, but I'd always thought the Carnival was where all the real fun was.

Hundreds of games and booths dotted a wide-open field ringed with a high wall, arches perforating the barrier at regular intervals. Acrobats and contortionists performed on high stages, moving their bodies in ways that just didn't seem possible.

Crazy rides clustered around the middle, gravity falls and rocket slides, spinners and zonks, and anything else that was guaranteed to make you scream.

"What was that?" Quinn asked.

"Barrier field," I explained. "Keeps the kiddos inside."

"Of course," he said blankly.

"I told you, people come to Rondi to have fun."

I headed off to the ticket booth and reached for my purse, then paused and waited.

"Thank you," Quinn acknowledged as he slid a credit chip into a slot I'd never even noticed before.

"I don't know why you're so funny about it," I said, still uneasy about someone spending credits on my behalf. "I'm the one taking you to all the fun places. This might not even be something you like."

"You're taking time out of your evening, showing me around," he shrugged, then waited for the machine to spit out two cards, loaded with the carnival's own currency. "And I know you're skipping out on part of your shift."

"You can't know that," I accused him. I mean, it was true. But there was no way he could have overheard me talking with Russar. Then something else distracted me. "You filled these things all the way up! There's no way we'll ever use all those tickets." I studied him through narrowed eyes. "Unless you really love the anti-g rides."

Quinn looked at the massive rides in the middle of the Carnival lot, watched the capsules as they were flung around the mag fields and shook his head.

"That might be a little too high adrenaline for me."

I thought about how fast he had moved, how it seemed like he'd just magically appeared on the top of the wall, grabbing me.

Saving me.

Somehow, I doubted there was anything here that was too scary for him.

"I'm going to just let that go. For now."

Courting couples shared piles of spun tolli, harried parents chased after children, and groups of young people tried their skills and luck at the games.

"I'm surprised to see so many families here," Quinn mused.

"Why?" I asked, trying to decide if I could fit another piece of tolli in with the two cones that were already happily in my tummy.

"I guess when somebody talks about a pleasure planet, I'm thinking of, well..." his quick glance towards me made my stomach do an uncomfortable flip.

And it wasn't just the cones.

"I guess I had assumed they're talking about other pleasures," he finished.

"Well, sure," I tried to get my tongue straightened out, my mouth suddenly, inexplicably dry.

"There's plenty of that kind of thing. Anything you'd want, really," I finally managed. "Almost. As long as everyone is willing, and old enough to sign a contract, it's all good here."

We passed another crowd of children, each wearing the wristband that would keep them inside the Carnival's boundaries, helping their parents track them when they ran off to find whatever mischief they could get up to inside.

"But people live here, work here, have families here. And even some of the visitors want to do something a little less...strenuous... sometimes."

We wandered further down the midway, just taking in the sights and sounds.

"Were you as wild as that?" Quinn pointed to another pack of kids, giggling as they stayed just a few steps ahead of their babysitter.

"Not exactly," I shrugged, looking over a booth where a wrinkled old man was deftly applying brilliantly multicolored temporary holotattoos.

"That's beautiful," I said, watching as he drew shimmering wings across the back of the teenage boy who lay face down on the table. "You're going to love it when he's done."

"Yeah," the kid remarked blandly. "We'll see what my mom says when I get home."

"Good luck," I offered, and we kept walking.

"I'm not from Rondi, and even when I was little, I didn't run around like that. Didn't have a chance."

He didn't say anything, didn't press, but still I felt the urge to explain.

"My aunt and uncles raised me, down on a tank farm at the tip of the southern continent."

Quinn looked surprised. "Hadn't really thought of this as a place for much in the way of farms."

"Seriously?" I shook my head. "All these people have to eat. That means a whole lot of replicators need to get stocked. And tank farming locally keeps the costs down. There's enough demand here for non-replicated food that there's even a few dirt farms." I wrinkled my nose. "Even if that just seems weird."

"Did you parents work on the farm, as well?" he asked, his tone just a little too casual.

I tried not to let it bother me. Void knew I was used to that sound.

"Nope, they died when I was a kid, left me with my mom's sister." I continued the spiel. At this point, I didn't even have to stop watching the darts game in the booth across the way. I'd told the story plenty of times. "Nice people, but never enough money. I got out of there as soon as I could."

The air between us chilled, grabbing my attention.

"Why did you need to leave quickly?" Quinn growled.

I stared at him, confused. His lips were pressed into a thin line, eyes narrowed.

Angry.

"What?" It finally clicked. "Oh, nothing like that, really." I bumped his arm with my shoulder, waiting for him to relax.

"My aunt and uncles are the sweetest people you'd ever meet. Just too many kids, not enough money."

His jaw clenched, then released. "Sorry," he admitted. "Some of the places I've been, there've been...issues."

It was sweet that he was worried.

A little paranoid, but sweet.

"They're good people. Not that I want to go back to

the farm anytime soon, but on good weeks with tips, I can usually send a little back to help them out."

And that was enough of that.

"Come on," I headed into the stream of people, "we need to play some of those games, burn through the tickets you bought."

We wandered through the crowds, but nothing caught my eye. Quinn seemed more amused than interested, but surely we'd find something he wanted to try his hand at.

And then I saw it.

"I need that," I pointed. "I've got to try to win it."

Scrolling across the top of the next booth were images of the prizes you could win.

Five points would get you any number of random little toys. Ten points gave options for various costume jewelry. But twenty...

Quinn followed where I was pointing.

"What in the Void is it?"

Blue and fuzzy, with long, floppy ears framing three giant, beseeching eyes.

It was perfect.

"It's a baby zuhair. It's adorable." I studied the game, figuring my odds. "We've got a set up like this in the back at the Merry Stormcloud. I can do this."

"I'm not going to stop you in your quest to get the whatever-the-hell," Quinn laughed.

I fed my card into the ticket reader and a rack of darts popped up. The targets floated back-and-forth, up and down, hovering in front of the backdrop.

"When it's slow, I practice. It's something to do, and every now and then, we get someone in who's willing to bet with me on a game. I'm not in a position to turn down money."

I threw, taking a straight-forward shot.

Guaranteed hit.

And the dart missed, sliding to the side of the target before clattering to the floor of the booth.

"What the—" I shook it off.

Different darts, different game.

Anyone could miss a warm-up shot.

I threw again. This time, it clipped the outer edge of the target, but still didn't rack up any points.

"Let's go find you another ugly thing to win," Quinn suggested. "I'm not sure this game can really be won."

"No," I insisted, frustrated now. "I want that madrik."

I finished the first rack, barely making five points.

I glared at the scoreboard.

"Want to keep going?" Quinn asked.

"Do you mind? It's just annoying," I explained.

"Far be it from me to stand between you and an obsession," he offered.

It wasn't an obsession. I just couldn't figure out why my throws were so off.

Sure, it had been too busy to practice lately, but I couldn't have gotten that bad, that quickly.

"I think the stupid thing's rigged," I muttered after I'd been no more successful with the second rack of darts.

Or the third.

Which was annoying, if not surprising.

Half the booths probably were adjusted just a bit to make more of a profit. Sure, the Carnival was supposed to be fun, but according to one of the old-timers I knew that worked in security, crooked games were part of the tradition.

And more profitable.

"Could be," Quinn said, and casually grabbed the last dart from the rack.

It didn't hit the target, but I couldn't see why not. It had flown straight and true, right towards the target.

Then it just slid to the side.

"Interesting," he said. "There's a glimmer, a light shimmer of blue just as the dart is about to hit. It almost reminds me..."

"Of what?" I asked, squinting at the background. "I don't see anything."

"It flashes in and out pretty fast," he said. "If I didn't know better, I'd say it was like the energy barrier used to keep the littles inside the Carnival area. How exactly does that work?"

At my shrug of bafflement, he turned to look at the archway we'd passed through on our way in.

"I'd bet that when the tracker in the wristband gets close enough to the arches, it signals the barrier to switch to full force by the time the kid gets there?"

I nodded. "It has to be something like that, yeah. I've been stuck on the wrong side a couple times, waiting for an adult to come and retrieve their kid."

"Then I guess we just have to be faster than the force field." Quinn put in his card, waited for the rack to pop open, then started to throw, his hand moving faster than I could process.

By the time I realized what was happening, he'd finished the entire rack of darts.

Not only had they all hit square in the bullseye, they were still there, each permasteel shaft quivering slightly from the force of the impact.

Usually, the dart struck and clung to the target just long enough for the points to be counted.

Then the target popped back out, pushing the dart to the grate in the floor, where a magnet pulled them down and prepped them for the chute where they'd be re-racked.

Not this time.

This time, the hovering, moving targets were pinned to the wall.

"Does that get your whatever-the-Void yet?" Quinn asked. "We might have to wait a while for someone to come by and reset the game."

"Yes, yes it does," I answered, slightly stunned.

The selector popped up, prompting me to select how I wanted to spend my twenty points.

And when the replicator had finished generating the doll, Quinn looked as startled as I felt. "It's as big as you are."

"Isn't it fabulous?" I gushed. "It's absolutely ridiculous, and I know exactly what I want to do with it."

"I will agree with one of those words," he said, eyebrows raised.

I hoisted the doll up to my hip, and the floppy head towered over me.

"Could you…"

"Sure," Quinn agreed, pushing one of the floppy ears out of my face.

"Thanks." I headed back through the crowd.

"Where to next?" he asked.

"Next," I said reluctantly, "we should probably get some dinner and head back. I traded tonight's shift with a friend, so I'll need to pick up hers tomorrow morning."

"Is the bar even open in the morning?" Quinn looked surprised.

"It's Rondi," I shrugged. "Nothing closes for long. Not when there's a chance to make money."

He'd learn, if he stayed here long enough.

"Profit trumps everything."

QUINN

"So, what do you want?" Trini asked.

What did I want?

The answer that sprang to my lips, even as she held that ridiculous stuffed doll, had to be hastily bitten back.

"What's your favorite place when you're off shift?" I answered instead.

She huffed slightly. "It's not very fancy. Probably not at all what you're used to."

"Do you want to go someplace fancy?" I asked quickly. Thinking about her past, how excited she'd been at such small treats as we'd had this evening, I cursed myself.

I should have looked at the damned brochure back

at the bar, found somewhere nice to take her for dinner.

She shook her head quickly, dashing all of those romantic thoughts away.

"Not really my scene, honestly. Besides, do you think they'd let me in looking like this?" she declined.

The city lights sparkled over her skin, and the warmth of her smile and the mischief in her eyes should have been a passport to anything, anywhere.

"Alright then, I'm not much for someplace dressy, if you're not. I'd have to think hard to remember my manners, anyway."

While Doc had made sure we had enough training and etiquette to pass almost anywhere, I'd be the first to admit I was a little rusty.

Maybe more than a little.

"Come on then, I know just the place. Nobody will look at you twice, manners or not."

I followed her through the crowd, thoughts spinning.

What was I doing here?

It was easy enough to say I was looking for traces of Torik.

That Trini had so far been the only possible lead.

But I should have asked around more, gone to other bars.

Surely there was a shadier side of town, and if Torik

had gone underground, it seemed that would be a more likely place to find him than the sections of town I'd visited with Trini.

But still, the evening hadn't been a waste.

I've been able to watch the crowds, seeing how people interacted here.

For a pleasure planet, there was a certain wariness. A certain tacit agreement that while fun might be the goal, sacrifices might have to be made for the collective good.

Like that crazy banking system.

If I didn't know better, I'd think that everyone owed the corporation for their livelihood and was paying it off.

It was surprising they didn't have to pay for their oxygen.

Maybe I should ask.

"Here we are, just down this way," Trini said, breaking me from my thoughts.

She turned quickly down a narrow street, then just as quickly backed up into me.

But not fast enough.

An earthshattering wail came from the little boy sprawled on the street in front of her.

"Oh my gosh, are you okay, honey?" Trini asked, kneeling next to him.

An exasperated looking man hurried to the child's

side. "He's fine, he just needs to learn to watch where he's going."

"But I ran into you. And I fell. And I tore my pants. And my knee hurts. And I'm gonna get in trouble!"

With every complaint, the child's voice grew higher and shriller.

"You know what would make it better?" Trini asked.

Big water-filled eyes blinked at her as the little boy shook his head back and forth, sniffling.

"Nothing."

"A new friend can make everything better," Trini promised, and handed him the giant doll.

Apparently she was right, because immediately the child clutched his new best friend and broke into a babbling explanation of how wonderful everything was now to his father.

The man picked the boy up, carefully balancing the doll, and headed out onto the Boulevard.

"I thought you really wanted that monstrosity," I commented softly as Trini watched them go.

"It's hard to be little sometimes," she whispered. "It seemed an easy enough fix." She shot me a mischievous grin. "Besides, if I really wanted another one, I know who to ask, right?"

I blinked, mulling that over as she skipped away. I caught up, then noticed the amazing smells coming from just a few doors away.

"Are we almost there?" The sudden growl of my belly made me hope that we were heading to wherever was the source of that aroma.

"Yep," Trini said, reaching an open doorway covered by a half-curtain. "Best empies in Rondi." She stepped through, and I followed.

"Best on Heladae or anywhere in the sector," a thin man insisted from behind the counter. "I guarantee it."

"Anything you don't like?"

I shook my head. "I suspect I could eat three of everything here," I admitted as my stomach let off another enormous rumble.

She shook her head sadly. "If you'd eaten all your cone, you wouldn't be so hungry now."

I handed her a credit chip and sat down at a small table, hand painted in a bright design of the three golden suns against a blue sky.

She joined me after a moment.

"He really does make the best empies in the city. Probably on the planet, too," she whispered.

"I believe you, but I don't know what that is. So it's an easy bet."

"Really?" Her eyes lit up. "I'm not going to tell you anything more. It's going to be a wonderful surprise."

I believed that, too. Because what I was smelling promised good things.

Within a few minutes, the thin man came back out

carrying a tray of bowls filled with small crispy half-moons of pastry, stuffed to bursting.

"And there's the dipping sauce," Trini explained as she picked up one of the golden pastries and carefully bit into the edge. "Careful, they're hot."

They were, and delicious.

Spicy and savory, with a cooling sweet sauce to be spooned into them.

For a moment, everything was silent as I focused on the food.

She pushed the third bowl towards me. "You really were hungry."

"I burned a lot of fuel," I said, then moved half the pastries onto my plate and pushed the bowl back towards her.

"No," she shook her head. "I'm done."

I ate the last few slowly, the initial ravenous hunger sated.

At least for food.

"If you're done, I should head back," Trini said, reluctance seeming to drag at her words.

"Is it dangerous at night?" I asked. "I was watching while we were walking, and I haven't seen any petty theft. Seems like there'd be plenty of opportunity for pickpocketing, if not flat out muggings."

She looked up in surprise. "Here? Not a chance. It'd be bad for business if anything like that was allowed to happen. Rondi City is probably the safest place you'll ever go."

No reason to tell her that wasn't exactly a high bar.

"No, Russar just worries about me. And," she blushed and looked down.

"And he doesn't trust me at all, does he?"

She bit her lip, shrugging helplessly. "It's just that he's protective. I've been working there a long time. He's got the whole big brother thing going on."

As long as that was all it was.

I caught myself. Really? I was here for information, moving on as soon as I had a solid lead.

Trini could partner up with Russar or anyone else, and it would be none of my business.

But it felt like my business.

"Come on, let's get you home before your big brother gets worried," was all I said as we headed into the brightly lit streets.

But even though we were back at the Merry Storm-cloud in less than half an hour, Russar didn't look as happy as we'd expected.

"I was hoping you'd stay out a little bit longer," he said.

"That's a first," Trini said, eyebrows raised. "What's going on?"

"You've got someone waiting for you in the back," Russar admitted. "With luck, they would've left before you returned." He scowled at me. "Couldn't you have taken her someplace further? Maybe come back in the morning?"

"I think you're forgetting, she's my guide," I answered. "It's her call where we go."

"Makkar's back again?" Trini sighed.

"This Makkar," I asked shortly. "The mopey-looking one that was here before?"

Trini stifled a laugh. "Yeah, that would be him."

Russar threw his hands up in the air. "Mopey, and needs to learn how to pull his weight. I get to say that. He's my little brother." He rested a hand on Trini's shoulder. "But it's not Makkar." He tilted his head back, just a bit. "It's Mada."

Trini went very still. "Mada Sommu?" she breathed. "What is she doing here?" "Looking for you," Russar said.

"For me?" she squeaked.

"Somebody want to catch me up on this?" I asked.

"Mada Sommu runs well, everything on Heladae," Trini explained in a whisper.

"Close enough to everything," Russar agreed. "And she is not afraid to do whatever it takes to keep her grip on things." He looked at Trini closely. "You can't think of any reason she'd be here?"

Trini shook her head, curls flying. "Nothing. Unless, unless it's something to do with Makkar."

"Better not keep her waiting," Russar decided. "She'll know you're back, I'm sure."

Trini swallowed hard, then headed to the back of the tavern. I moved to follow her, but Russar put a hand out.

"You're just passing through, no reason to get involved in this."

"Is Trini involved?" I asked softly, trying to remember that Trini considered this man an older brother.

And therefore not someone I should throw through a wall.

"Apparently," Russar admitted.

"Then I think I'll go see what's happening," I said mildly and moved past him.

I lengthened my strides and reached Trini's side by the time she stopped at a table where a woman with long red hair appeared to be holding court.

Three toughs, dressed in obvious battle armor, were ranged behind her.

The one to the left stepped forward as I reached Trini's side, but froze when the woman, obviously Mada Sommu, raised her hand.

"Not yet, darling. Let's see what this is."

I grinned. "As far as I'm concerned, *this* isn't anything." Slipping an arm around Trini's waist, I pulled her into my side. "Just checking up on my girl."

"Really?" the woman drawled. "Then maybe you're just as interested as I am in this question."

She turned back to Trini, who shivered a little under my hand. "What was Makkar doing here earlier today?"

Trini shook her head. "I don't know, he comes by sometimes, but I promise, I'm not seeing him. We broke up long before you guys started, well...dating?"

Mada laughed, long and low. "Dating is a word for it. You think he just comes by for old times' sake?"

"I think he tries to borrow money from Russar sometimes," Trini admitted. "He's not worth much, but Russar's not going to let his little brother be out of credits."

"And that's really all he came by for?" the woman asked again, her piercing cold green eyes moving back and forth from me to Trini.

"That's all I know about, ma'am." Trini nodded. "He might have been planning to meet someone here, but I didn't see him talking with anyone else."

"Well, then, that's enough for now." The woman rose and her guards snapped into formation around her, then they strode out of the Merry Stormcloud without a backward glance.

Trini sagged against me and I put her in the chair. "What's wrong," I asked. "Do you know what that guy was here for?"

She shook her head. "No idea. Just, that woman is scary," she whispered.

Russar rushed over, handed her a small glass of clear sparkly liquid. "Figured you could use this."

"I think she's after Makkar," Trini told him, and took a sip.

"Can't imagine why she'd bother," Russar said. "He's pretty enough to catch a girl's eye, even yours, and you should've known better. But I told him from the beginning, she would chew him up and spit him out if he stepped wrong."

I rubbed Trini's shoulders. "She doesn't seem like the kind of woman to go chasing after a man."

"She's not," Trini agreed. "But if she thought someone had disrespected her, hurt her? She'd chase after that, all right."

"Well, nothing to do with us," Russar announced. "It's quiet and Paulo's out of town. I might go ahead and close down, restock and clean for a while. You head up to bed, and I'll see you in the morning."

He headed back to the bar, but I stayed where I was, frozen.

"What did he mean for you to head up to bed?" I said slowly. "With me?"

The frightened look finally left Trini's face as she rolled her eyes. "Of course not. I live here, too. It's cheap, and you can't beat the commute."

Oh. Of course she did. But the fire that had sparked in my blood refused to die down as I followed her up the narrow stairway, eyes hungrily devouring her curves.

"See, this is my room right here." She stopped at the doorway before mine.

She'd be on the other side of the thin wall. All night.

"Thanks for letting me play tour guide," she smiled up at me. "Not sure if that helped you with what you were looking for, but it was a lot of fun."

I couldn't help it. I slid one hand over her hip and drew her to me. Bending towards her upturned face, I kissed her temple, then brushed the edge of her ear, waiting for her small hands to push against my chest, to resist.

Listening for the smallest breath of 'no'.

But instead, she stretched up on her toes. "I think you missed," she whispered, then my lips fell on hers.

I'd meant to only take a taste, a brief good night kiss, a sample of what I couldn't have.

But as she melted against me, my tongue teased the seam of her lips until she opened, soft and sweet.

And for a change, this was a sweetness I'd never have enough of, never be sated.

With every strength of will I'd ever possessed, I let her go and stared at the wall, fighting to control my breath.

"Good night, Trini."

I walked further down the hall and waited by my door until she entered her room.

I stretched out on the bed, waiting for sleep, but as usual, it didn't come.

Instead, when I closed my eyes, I saw my console back on our old ship, where I'd decoded the distress call so long ago.

Convinced my brothers we had to detour from our mission, investigate.

Where I'd brought us all into a trap, to be slaughtered by the Hunters' games, then put into a dreamless sleep, until we were woken by Nadira and Ronan.

I didn't sleep much anymore.

Over and over the images played out, and no matter how much I tried, I was powerless to change them. To stop myself from trusting that message.

Crash.

I sat up halfway. I'd been so wrapped up in the past that it took a moment for the sounds to detangle, to separate reality from memory.

Thud.

A fight.

Here and now, not on the ship. Not on the *Star*.

And then a scream.

Trini.

TRINI

Long after I heard Quinn's door close, I sat on my bed, knees hugged to my chest in the dark room.

My lips still burned.

Nothing had ever felt like that, had sent a flame of desire through my body with just a kiss.

Nothing.

No one had made me want like that, had made me hungry.

When he broke away, I'd almost begged him to continue.

But he would only be here for a few days, then gone.

Quinn had been very clear.

And I'd be left alone, hurting and broken.

I couldn't do it.

I touched my lips again, almost able to still taste him, feel his tongue tangled with mine.

I couldn't do it. I'd never survive.

The building creaked and I shook myself.

If I was smart, I'd get ready for bed instead of staring blankly out into the darkness.

Morning would come before I was ready, and if Russar had decided to clean and restock, he really meant it.

He'd want every surface scrubbed and decontaminated before we reopened.

Sure, it needed to be done, but for every hour it took us, he'd push even harder.

"We're losing money!" he'd call out as we pushed as fast as we could to finish the job.

Maybe being busy would be a good thing.

Maybe I would notice less when Quinn left.

I scoffed, stretched, and reached for the covers.

Then the world exploded.

The window crashed in, covering the bed with tiny pieces of plexi, at the same moment that my door burst open.

I shrieked, scrabbling back towards the headboard.

"Who are you? What do you want?"

But the three bulky forms stayed silent, their obsidian armor shifting and flowing in the shadows, strong arms ending in long, taloned gauntlets, black masks covering their faces completely.

One reached towards me and I flinched away from those sharp claws as they raked through the shoulder of my dress, cutting it to ribbons.

"No!" I screamed, grabbing the small vase of flowers from next to my bed and hurling it with all my strength.

The attacker dodged easily, but it bought me a moment.

Unfortunately, I'd need longer than a moment to get out of this.

Another black-suited goon reached for me from the other side of the bed and I swung towards him with the zuhair statuette, crashing it over his head.

He didn't even stumble.

My breath caught in my chest, ears ringing as I tried to think.

I'd run out of things to throw, out of places to hide, out of places to go.

There was nothing to save me.

Then the door crashed open again, and Quinn was there.

"Careful!" I shouted, but he was already moving, flowing like quicksilver.

He grabbed the nearest attacker and threw him over the bed to smash against the wall. Before that one hit the floor, he spun and struck a blow to the chin of the second, so hard I could hear the snap of the man's neck as his head rocketed back.

The third grabbed me, dragging me towards the broken window as I struggled and kicked.

"Let her go," Quinn snarled.

The masked intruder and I both froze.

That low growl wasn't completely a human voice.

I recovered faster, attempting to push away from my kidnapper, still caught in his grip.

Quinn vaulted over the bed, feet catching square in the chest of the man who held me.

As he stumbled back, Quinn tore me from his arms and kicked his chest again, harder this time.

The third man fell through the window, to crash on the pavement below.

"Are you all right?" Quinn demanded, ignoring the damage to the room around us, the two bodies on the floor.

"Trini, I need you to answer me." There'd been no fear on his face when he fought.

It was there now, in his eyes as he searched my expression for any clues to my state of mind.

"I'm fine," I finally croaked.

"Are you certain?" he pressed, fingers suddenly gentle as he touched the torn top of my dress. "They didn't hurt you, didn't do anything?"

"They didn't have a chance, you were here so fast," I breathed.

"Good." He held me to him tightly, and for a brief moment I had the strangest notion he was smelling my hair, breathing in my scent. The tension flowed out of him slowly, then he stepped back.

"Grab your things, I don't think it's safe here."

Then he stopped, head tilted as if hearing something I couldn't.

"Who else do you think is coming?" I challenged him, balking at the thought of leaving my room, my home.

"I don't know, and I don't want to be here to find out."

Steel laced his words, and I realized he was right.

"I need to change," I said awkwardly, suddenly horribly aware of how much of my chest was showing through the torn dress.

Quinn nodded, turning his back stiffly as I quickly tore off the ruined dress and pulled on pants, a long-sleeved shirt, and boots.

"All right, you can turn back now."

He nodded in approval of my choice of clothing. "What else do you want to take?"

"There's not much left," I explained.

"I'll be right back," he said, and before I could ask

where he was going, he'd returned, his bag slung over one shoulder.

Walking over to the broken window, he looked down. "It won't be a lot of fun, but just close your eyes and hold on tight."

"Wait a minute, what?" I gasped. "We can't go out the window. Besides, we need to check on Russar. One of those guys came up the stairs. What if he tried to stop them?"

Quinn's shoulders slumped as he turned away from the window. "I'm going to regret this. Come on."

As we approached the stairs, I heard the noise, too.

A soft, wet gasping sound.

"What is that...Oh, no!" I exclaimed, pushing my way past Quinn to hurry down the rest of the stairs.

Russar's body sprawled a third of the way up, each step slick with blood from the wound across his belly.

I knelt next to him, trying to remember an ancient first aid vid my uncles had insisted we all watch back at the tank farm.

"Do I press?" I asked Quinn. "Do you have something that would stop the bleeding? I don't know what to do!"

He rubbed his eyes, then pulled out a spare shirt from his bag. "It will help a little," he said, tearing it into strips. "I don't usually carry a med kit. It's not really useful."

"We've got to take him someplace, got to get him help." I couldn't remember the name of the young medtech Russar had called last year when I'd dropped a full tray on my foot. Terro, Torre, something like that.

"Get me to Doctor Jaylan," Russar whispered, almost too soft to hear.

"I don't know anyone named that," I sobbed. "Can I call Paulo, would he know?"

Russar shook his head slowly. "Don't involve him. Get to the Fourth Quarter, ask anyone for the healer. They'll know."

"Please," I looked up to Quinn, his face impassive. "Please help me. Help him."

He sighed, handed me his bag, and more carefully than I imagined possible, lifted Russar's massive form into his arms.

"Lead on, let's go find this healer."

As we slipped out the back door of the Merry Stormcloud, Quinn paused in the doorway. "Is everything in this city lit up like a battlefield?" he asked.

I looked at him sharply. "I... don't know. I've never seen one."

"If there are back ways, I think it would be a good idea. Those guys probably had trackers on them. Their handler will know when they've failed the mission." He glanced down at Russar, lying limp in his arms.

I couldn't see him breathing, but had to believe he was.

"Another wave will be on our trail, soon."

"Right." I hugged the bags to my chest, forced my breathing to slow, and thought about the best way to the Fourth Quarter. Not the fastest, but what might be the darkest.

"This way."

"I guess we can consider this an extension of your tour," I muttered as we headed into another back street. The residential zones tended to be quieter, darker.

After the first few moments, I stopped looking back to check that Quinn was following me. He'd stayed a constant three paces behind me, carrying Russar's body as if the big man weighed nothing.

"The First Quarter is the Carnival, the Boulevard and the adjacent streets. All the places that people who come to Rondi want to visit, all the best restaurants and galleries."

I paused, holding my breath as a laughing trio of women crossed in front of us, moving on towards the lights, then resumed.

They hadn't seen us, hadn't noticed anything other than their own good time.

It wasn't that long ago that Risti and I had been out on an evening just like that.

This was nothing like it. What hadn't we seen then?

"The Second Quarter is for the people who create the things that are sold in the shops. Craftsmen, artisans. Not the famous virtuosos who attract a crowd just to watch them create works of beauty, but solid professionals, nonetheless."

I couldn't even hear Quinn, just had to trust he was still there.

Trust he still held Russar.

Trust that Russar breathed, could be saved by whoever this mysterious Jaylan was.

"The Third Quarter is where people who work in the cheaper shops live, the ones who repair the cleaning bots, service the replicators, all the details of life that no one seems to remember, but the city wouldn't run without them."

The darkness here, so far from the First Quarter, was heavier, almost tangible. No sounds of the constant party of Rondi, but something else touched the air. Something threatening.

"What's the Fourth Quarter," Quinn asked.

"Everything else," I answered. "Everything that can't be classified, the people that no one wants to deal with, but even Mada can't find a way to purge the quarter forever."

"Finally," Quinn breathed, "something a little less wholesome. I was beginning to worry."

"What?" I stopped, shocked enough to finally turn

back to stare at him, but then someone stepped out of the shadows.

"You're new around here, friend."

I bit my lip, hunching over the bags I still clung to.

But the man wasn't talking to me.

"Is that a problem?" Quinn asked flatly.

"I don't know, could be," the first man said.

The darkness shifted, as more men stepped out, surrounding us.

These weren't like the men who had attacked me in my room.

Most were tall, but even in the dim light, I could see their clothes were torn, ragged. No armor. No masks.

It didn't make them any less terrifying.

"Please," I said, interrupting whatever testosterone-fueled nightmare was about to start. "We're looking for a man. Doctor Jaylan. He's going to help us."

"Really?" the first man looked at me, startled. "That old man doesn't do anyone any good, not without reason. Especially not someone bleeding as much is your friend there."

"Still," Quinn said. "He asked that we take him to this Jaylan. So here we are."

One of the other men stepped closer to Quinn's side, close enough to get a look at who he was carrying.

"Hey," he called out. "It's the Rough Man!" His nostrils flared at the sight of the bloodsoaked makeshift bandages across Russar's gut. "Venac, this guy knifed the Rough Man!"

Even in the darkness, I could see Quinn roll his eyes. "Of course, and now I'm hauling him around to take him to the doctor. Because that's how it always works when you stab someone," he snapped.

"Are you the one that did this?" the first man demanded angrily.

"No, I'm the one who's been carrying him for an hour through your damn city. Do you know where this doctor is or not? Because honestly, I don't think he's going to last much longer."

I stepped between the two men. "Russar is my friend," I begged. "Don't let him die while you fight."

Finally, the leader backed down. "Come on, you're almost there."

We ducked through back alleys, turning and twisting so quickly I was sure they were trying to make sure we wouldn't be able to find our way back.

"If you're lucky, the old man will be in shape to help."

The man stopped in front of a rusted door and banged his fist on it. "Open up, old man, are you high or deaf? You've got a patient."

I waited, ears pricked for every sound, until I heard a shuffling step. Finally, the slide and click of metal as locks were released, one by one down the length of the door.

"What you want now, you hooligans?"

When the man stepped closer, I bit back a cry of horror.

Tall, almost as tall as Quinn but thin to the point of being spindly, the old man swung his head from side to side as if trying to determine who had disturbed him.

A shock of wiry gray hair haloed his face, but his eyes were what caught my attention.

Or rather, the lack of them.

Twin black plexi lenses curved around the eye sockets from the brow to the cheekbones.

"What do you want, Missy," he snapped. "Come to talk? Or just stare and point?"

"Are you Jaylan?" I blurted. "Dr. Jaylan? Russar said that you could help."

"That's a name I haven't heard in a while, how's the kid doing?"

"Not particularly well," Quinn said, and stepped closer.

As the doctor leaned over to peer at the very still form, blue lights flashed across the plexi lenses.

"Well, you'd better bring him in." He straightened up. "Can't examine him properly out here." Jaylan turned to reenter the building.

"Been a long time since you worked on a fighter,

Doc. Still got the touch?" One of the men called out, and for a moment, I thought I saw Quinn stiffen.

"We'll see," was the only answer.

"What do we get out of it?" the leader of the gang asked. "We guided them here, and you get a client out of it, right? So what do we get?"

Jaylan's voice came from deep inside the building. "Two rounds of stitching up."

"Five," the man shouted back.

"Three, and count yourself lucky."

That seemed to suffice because, with a quick nod, the gang faded back into the darkness.

"In we go," Quinn said, and followed the doctor into the building. I scurried after him, not wanting to be left outside.

This wasn't my Rondi City. Of course, I'd known that it wasn't all a never-ending party. Lots of people worked hard to make sure the glitter stayed bright.

But here in the Fourth Quarter, there was nothing of the magic, nothing that tied it to what I knew or understood.

Throat tight, my own breathing too loud in my ears, I kept Quinn's broad back in my sights. Sporadic lights made a path through the building, one vast room stretching into the darkness.

It smelled sour, stale.

Finally, we reached a section that was more brightly

lit than its surroundings. Racks of equipment surrounded three counters and a pair of permasteel tables.

"Put the boy here," Jaylan ordered, pointing to one of the tables.

Quinn carefully lowered the body and stepped back.

I couldn't take it anymore. Russar was so still, I couldn't see his chest move at all. And there was so much blood...

"Did he die?" I whispered. "Did I take too long to get us here?"

Quinn came to my side and pulled me into his chest. "I promise I didn't carry a body all that way. He's still alive." Quinn paused. "Barely."

Jaylan was already poking and prodding at the wound, my clumsy bandages torn off, cast aside on the floor. "This is deep, nasty. He's lost a lot of blood." The lenses flashed blue again as he studied the injury. "It'll take more than just a transfusion or two to get him back on his feet."

The old man straightened up. "I'm going to be burning through supplies on this. What will it get me?"

"Name your price," Quinn answered. "As long as you can take credit chips."

The man laughed. "Do I look like I have a bank account? No, what favor can you do for me? What can you trade?"

Quinn's arm tightened around me, and Jaylan laughed. "Get your hackles down, boy. She's far too young for me."

Quinn studied the doctor. "You fix him up, get him good as new, I can introduce you to someone who can fix your eyes."

"There's nothing left to fix, boy." Jaylan curled his lip, baring yellow-stained teeth. "That bitch, Mada, burned them out. I've got the interface routed directly to what's left of the nerves."

"Still, I know someone who can give you new organic eyes," Quinn shrugged. "If you can do her a favor in turn, she might even keep your display overlays."

"Impossible," Jaylan snapped. "To rebuild organic eyes, to rebuild the nerves, they'd have to—"

He broke off as Quinn squeezed my shoulder and stepped into the light, letting it fall clearly on him.

The lenses flashed blue again for a long moment.

"Well," Jaylan said, "if someone can do that, maybe they can fix something like me."

"You'd have to travel out of the sector," Quinn said. "She's not coming here."

"I'll have somebody come by to water the house-plants," Jaylan answered distractedly, completely focused now on Russar. "The two of you, shut up and get out of my way. I've got work to do."

QUINN

This was where I needed to be.

It was a good bet Jaylan was an unlicensed medtech, but he seemed to know what he was doing.

If Torik was on this planet, the Fourth Quarter was the place to start asking questions.

I glanced at Trini. Her face was pale as she watched the doctor work.

"I don't see how anyone could survive losing so much blood," she muttered.

The old man saved me from having to answer.

"Wouldn't be the first time this boy has needed me to patch him up," Jaylan snapped.

"How do you know each other?" Trini wondered, obviously struggling to reconcile her friend with this part of town. "And why did those men know Russar? Why did they call him that other name?"

I found a mostly cleaned-off counter, perched, and pulled her into my lap, wrapping my arms around her.

"Are you sure you want those answers?" I asked softly. "Sometimes people's lives are, well, complicated."

She shot me an angry glance. "I can handle complicated things." She turned back to the table where Jaylan worked. "What I can't handle is being lied to."

"Young people, so quick to see things in black and white," Jaylan said as he pulled over what looked like a home-rolled cellular regenerator and clamped it to the table, so that it could roll back and forth over the worst of the wound.

"Doubt if the boy ever lied to you, you just didn't ask the right questions. And maybe he didn't want to go back there." The high-pitched hum of the regenerator filled the room and I fought the urge to cover my ears.

"Go back where?" Trini questioned.

"The fighting pits."

There was more, but for a moment, I lost track of place and time, lost track of everything.

The fighting pits. How could Russar have been there?

I got a quick grip on myself.

Ridiculous. Of course they didn't mean the Hunters, the *Star*.

Just the same sort of shows of brutality and skill that humans had brought to every planet, licensed or not.

Jaylan was still talking.

"So that's how he got the money to open up that place of his," he finished. "He was smart, didn't hang on to the persona of Rough Man Russar for so long that he started losing."

Trini's lips curved up in a soft smile. "No wonder he didn't feel the need to keep bouncers on staff. I wonder how many of our patrons already knew. We certainly have less trouble than some of the other bars."

"Could be," Jaylan said.

"Hmm, that's not good," he muttered, peering closely at the side of the wound, augmented lenses flickering so quickly I could no longer make out the readings.

"This is gonna be a tricky bit," Jaylan said. "You kids get out of here. Let me work in peace."

"But," Trini protested, "what if he wakes up? Somebody should tell his husband what's going on."

"You're not gonna be able to do any good here, kid," Jaylan said. "And Paulo won't either. Just worry himself sick."

He turned to look at me. "If trouble is after you, I don't want it here. Come back in a day or two. But I'm going to hold you to that deal."

I stood and set Trini on her feet. Taking her small

bag and tucking it into mine, I slung it over my shoulder and laced my fingers with hers.

"Actually, the person you'd want to see would be disappointed if I didn't give her a chance to play with what you've done to yourself. We'll be back."

Trini was silent as we made our way back out of the building, and I braced for the questions I knew she must have.

But all she said was "Where do we go now?"

"You're the tour guide, remember?"

She was silent, worried, one hand pressed to her neck.

"But we could really use some information," I continued. "Do you know anyone who might have any ideas on why you were attacked?"

She laughed nervously as we headed out of the Fourth Quarter. No one bothered us, but I could feel the eyes on my back.

"I work in a bar," she finally answered. "I save my tips, send as much home as I can, and once a month go out for a splurge night with Risti. Mostly we end up trying to win gaudy trinkets at the Carnival after having too many trakkos. That's about it, I'm afraid." She ran a hand through the tangle of her hair. "It's not a very exciting life. Certainly not something that would lead to masked men in black trying to abduct me."

"It can't be a coincidence that it came so soon after Mada's visit," I mused. "Do you know anyone who might have an in with her? Let us know what she's thinking, why she was interested in you?"

"Makkar might know," her voice dripped with derision. "He's been her plaything for almost a year. But I wouldn't trust him to give me the straight story on anything."

"To be honest, it sounded like even Russar didn't think much of him," I answered.

The streets were lighter now, the residential hives tidier.

"Risti might have heard something at work tonight," Trini said slowly. "She does tend to hear almost everything eventually."

"Where does she work? Let's start there."

"Momma Deese's. Which is probably exactly what it sounds like." Trini laughed. "But she wouldn't thank us for showing up in the middle of her shift. Her clients might find it a little distressing."

"That's a good point. And sounds a little more public than we want to be right now."

"She should be home in a few hours," Trini continued. "We'll have to wait."

And if she didn't have the information we needed, I could always head back to the Fourth Quarter.

I was pretty sure that someone there would have the information we needed.

Even if they needed a little convincing.

But this way might be faster.

We crossed the city in silence.

"That's her hive," Trini said. "Usually if I'm meeting her, I wait over there." She pointed to a well-lit, cozy-looking café. Tables edged out onto the walkway and blooming flowers in a profusion of colors spilled from wide planters and hanging baskets.

"It looks nice," I agreed. "It also looks pretty crowded."

Trini nodded. "And they'd recognize me. If someone really is after me for some reason, it probably wouldn't be the smartest idea." She laughed. "It's a pity, I really could use one of their kafs about now."

"What about over there?" I asked, pointing to a dark patch of overgrowth halfway down the block. "What is that?"

"It's actually a pretty little park, but the lady who used to keep it tidy died a few months ago," Trini said. "Risti and a few of the others have been trying to get a group together to get it back in hand, but no one seems to have enough time. It looks pretty awful now, doesn't it?"

"Actually, it looks perfect."

And it was.

Just a thin slice of a block, and even I could tell that whoever the woman was who'd claimed this bit of land as her own had done a good job turning it into a miniature park.

Trini led the way through the darkness and I listened closely for any signs of other visitors in the deep cover.

"It's strange after all the chaos and lights and activity of your city," I said. "I think this is the first quiet place I've found."

Trini brushed off the seat of an old metal bench, the low-hanging branches of a bright flowering tree curved overhead, almost entirely blocking us from view.

"I think that's why the old lady did it," she said. "It's not exactly profitable, but it's nice having a bit of peace."

I sat near her, tucking our bags by my feet.

Trini wrapped her arms tight around her abdomen, staring into the darkness.

"Tell me about how you met Russar," I requested, hoping to get her mind off the situation.

There was the briefest flash of a grin. "It was actually Paulo, Russar's husband, who found me. I was such an idiot when I came to town. Thought I'd get a job easy, be rich. Isn't that what people do in the city?"

I didn't say anything, just stretched an arm across

the back of the bench and rubbed the tight spot between her shoulder blades.

"Most places you apply want you to have a skill already, you know?" She slowly relaxed against my hand. "It's not that strange when I think about it, but I hadn't. And really, no one here needed a scrawny teenager that only knew how to work a growing vat. Didn't have much in the way of social skills yet, either."

"What did you do?" I asked, curious.

"You gotta know, I don't think twice about what Risti does for a living." Trini shot me a quick peek from the corner of her eye. "She thinks it's fun, even has her favorite clients. But even then, I didn't think I would enjoy it."

Carefully, I focused on the hand rubbing soothing circles on her back while the other one clenched into a fist around the metal side of the bench.

"But I'd pretty much made up my mind that it was either that or go hungry, but then…" She trailed off and a growl threatened to break free from my control.

"Then what," I prompted as calmly as I could.

"Paulo found me," she laughed. "I'd been pacing back and forth in front of one of the brothels, no place near as nice as Momma Deeses's, trying to get my courage up." She shook her head, embarrassed. "He said he'd seen me when he went in and I was still there when he came out, and obviously something was wrong."

"I thought he was Russar's husband?"

"What?" She looked confused. "Oh no, he wasn't visiting for himself, he's a mechanic. The replicator had gotten stuck, and apparently one of the rooms had been flooded with banana pudding." She giggled. "I never did ask for details."

"He bought me kaf and a sandwich and watched as I inhaled the whole thing. He asked what I knew how to do, and I told him not much, other than follow orders and lift heavy things."

I took a deep breath, relaxed, and hoped I hadn't bent the metal too much.

"He took me to the Merry Stormcloud and told Russar that he'd found a new waitress. That was," she thought back, "almost ten years ago."

"They sound like good people. Kind."

"I didn't think so at first," she admitted. "Russar can be a serious taskmaster. I think I spent more time memorizing our menu and what the customers wanted than I did sleeping that first month."

She trailed off. "What if he doesn't make it? How am I ever going to explain what happened to Paulo?"

"Hey, hey," I pushed her hair out of her face. "I know Jaylan didn't look like much, but I suspect he's dealt with more than a few stabbings in his time. Russar'll be fine. And we're working to find out what's going on, get it straightened out."

She turned her face up, eyes searching my face.

"I'm scared," she whispered.

I ran my hand down the curve of her cheek, felt the delicate skin of her throat, and breathed in the scent of her.

"I'm not letting anything happen to you," I promised.

The words rang true through my very core.

I could no more let anything happen to her than cut off my own right hand.

At the beginning, the kiss was no more than a brush against her lips, but slowly she stole her hands upwards, fingers twining into my hair, and I groaned against her lips.

"Trini," I murmured, pulling her tightly against me.

Lightly, she pivoted towards me until she was kneeling on the bench, straddling my lap.

"Everything is crazy," she whispered in between kisses. "I don't understand what's going on." Another kiss, another step towards oblivion.

I rained kisses down her neck towards the chaste neckline of her shirt.

"But I know I want you, want this."

My fingers dug into the curve of her hip as she clung to me.

"I don't know what's going on either, and it doesn't matter," I growled. "We'll face it and finish it. Together."

So lost in the madness of her touch, I nearly didn't

hear the sharp click of heels on the pavement approaching our hidden nook.

I stood quickly, slipping her onto the bench and standing between her and the street.

"Oh my goodness," Trini said, her breathing still fast, a little frantic. "It's Risti, she's home already."

Lousy timing, I snarled to myself. But probably for the best. A few more moments and nothing would have stopped us.

"Let's wait, be certain it's her," I whispered to Trini.

I grabbed our bags and she laced her fingers with mine and followed me to the edge of the overgrown square. "Oh yeah, can't mistake that hair for anyone else's," Trini laughed softly.

It was true. The young woman did have an impressive length of hair, at the moment all pulled tightly into a high ponytail.

Suddenly I recognized her. "Isn't that the woman who was dancing at your bar earlier? I thought you said she worked…elsewhere?"

"Think of it as a hobby," Trini said, tugging me towards the building.

I scoured the street, listening for any signs of intruders, but no one had followed the woman.

"Risti!" Trina whispered urgently.

The woman froze in the doorway, then spun towards us. "Girl, what have you gotten yourself into?"

she demanded. Quickly she swiped the door open. "Get inside, quick."

As I passed by her, she fixed me with a narrow glare.

"If I find out this is all your fault, we're going to have words, buddy."

TRINI

The elevator in Risti's hive worked, unlike the one in the Merry Stormcloud, which was a fine thing considering her apartment was on the 35th floor of the hive.

Quinn took up half the space of the elevator car, even though he pressed back into the far corner.

Risti tucked her arm inside of mine. "Honey, I've got to know what's happening. People are—"

Quinn shook his head. "Could we wait a few moments? I'd like to check something out."

Risti huffed impatiently and I wondered what Quinn was thinking. We needed her on our side.

When she palmed us into her room, Quinn reached inside his bag, coming out with a small black wand and painstakingly running it across each wall, then the floors and ceilings, as if painting with invisible ink.

"Looks like we're clean," he said, putting the device back in his bag.

"What did you think?" Risti snapped. "That I had bugs in here? That I would betray my friend?"

"No. I thought that from what Trini would say, just in casual conversation, it wouldn't be hard for anyone to know you were friends." He paused at the sight of the small sofa and eyed it warily, finally deciding prudence was the better option and sitting cross-legged on the floor. "If I knew that in one day, what would other people who have been here longer, had ears to the ground on this planet for longer, have figured out?"

Risti paled, just a little, then nodded sharply." You're right. We have to play it smart." Hurrying over to the one window, she slapped on the privacy screen. "I haven't done much with the place, but you can bet I spent the money on decent screens."

"Now," she drew me down next to her on the sofa. "Tell me everything."

It didn't take long. We didn't know much.

"We came back from just sightseeing, and Mada was there, asking about Makkar."

"Having Mada's interest is never a good thing," Risti said.

"I gathered that," Quinn commented. "We met a

gentleman tonight who would put it a little more strongly than that, honestly."

"But she didn't say anything, just asked what he'd been by for this morning," I argued. "And I don't know anything!"

"I believe you, honey" Risti leaned forward to hug me. "You're not exactly secret agent material."

"And then…" my voice shook and I blindly reached my hand towards Quinn.

He took it, wrapping his massive fingers around mine. "Someone broke into her room," he answered for me. "Three someones." His voice deepened and he squeezed my hand reassuringly. "They were trying pretty hard to take her."

"And, and I broke the zuhair," I interrupted. "I threw it at them, and it didn't do a damn bit of good, but it broke anyway." Just thinking about the shattered pieces on the floor made my throat close again.

"Oh honey," Risti said. "We'll go win another one, just as soon as all this is over."

"As long as I'm not there for it," Quinn muttered.

"Then we found Russar, and brought him to a doctor, and well, now we're here," he finished the story.

"I couldn't think of anywhere else to go."

"I'm glad you came," Risti said. "There hasn't been anything said in the open, but the whispers are that

Mada's looking for you and Makkar, that he stole something from her, and she's furious."

"But I don't have anything to do with Makkar!" I threw my hands up in the air and stood from the sofa to pace. I needed to move, needed something, anything, to make sense.

"Every few months, he comes by the bar, gets a free drink from his brother, and probably asks for a loan. Hassles me a little, I remind him we're not getting back together, then he goes and everyone is happy again."

"I know that," Risti said. "But apparently I'm not the one who needs to be convinced."

"I don't want to have to convince Mada," I insisted. "I wouldn't even know where to start."

A soft beep interrupted my complaint.

It came again and I realized it was coming from Quinn's bag.

"Is there a bug after all?" I wondered.

"No, just a comm." He tilted his head towards the open door to the bedroom. "Mind if I step away for a minute?"

"Say one word about my housekeeping and I'm kicking you out," Risti said.

She probably was kidding. Maybe.

He grabbed his bag and stepped inside, and no matter how hard I strained my ears, I couldn't hear anything but his muffled voice.

"All right, quick!" Risti said. "Tell me the rest of it."

"There really isn't any more to it." I scrubbed my hands over my face. "You know everything I do, and it just isn't much."

"Is this his fault?" she demanded. "Did he do something that dragged you into this?"

I blinked, surprised. "I can't imagine how. He just got here. And Makkar showed up earlier today, before Quinn even came into the bar."

"Maybe..." she mused. "So tell me what you know. Not about Mada, or Makkar. About him." Her face lit up with glee. "I should have made you bet me earlier today. You would have owed me so many credits."

"Well," my cheeks burned and suddenly I couldn't meet her eyes. "He might be interested."

"Yessss," Risti coaxed me onward.

"And I might be interested, too," I admitted.

"I can't imagine how you could not be," she said dryly. "He's a pretty interesting package."

"But it's more complicated than that." I started pacing again.

How much did I know about him? I wondered.

Anything at all?

What had Doctor Jaylan seen when he had looked at Quinn, scanned him through those strange sensors that had replaced his eyes?

"He's not here for long. It would be foolish for me to

start anything."

Risti jumped up from the sofa and strode over to me, grabbing my shoulders. "Girl, it would be foolish for you not to do anything. I know you hate getting hurt, but you've got to risk a little." She shook me, just a tiny bit. "It took me two years to even get more than a hello out of you. You can't keep everybody out forever."

"I don't keep you out," I grumbled. "Or Russar. Or Paulo."

"We don't count," she said doggedly. "Not like this. Sit back down, I need to make a call."

A half smile crossed her face as she flicked her fingers over her commtab.

"There. That's handled, at least."

"What's handled?" Quinn asked as he came back in the room.

"We need a plan. Or at least, you do," Risti said. "You two need to find a way to get out of town. And I need to let you guys plan in peace."

She stood up, headed to the bedroom, and returned in a few minutes, makeup refreshed, hair curled, and a teal overnight bag over her shoulder.

"Just in case anyone is following me, I'm gonna go spend some quality time with a client. He's been pestering me about it for weeks. I'll have fun." She shot me a wide-eyed stare. "Maybe you guys should have some fun, too."

Sneaking a glance at Quinn, I was glad to see I wasn't the only one who was blushing.

On the way to the door, Risti marched over to Quinn and poked her forefinger into his chest.

"And you take care of her, understand?"

"I'm planning to," Quinn said mildly. "You're a good friend."

"And a terrible enemy."

And with that, Risti slid the door shut behind her.

And I was alone in the apartment.

With Quinn.

"We should probably get some rest." He cleared his throat. "Making plans when tired often doesn't go well."

"Sure," I said.

It made sense.

Except I wasn't tired at all.

"You take the bed, I'll be fine on the couch"

"You've got to be kidding me." I looked between Quinn and the tiny couch. "I don't think you could even sit on the thing, much less stretch out."

"I was planning to move the pillows to the floor. It'll be fine." He smiled, and all the severity of his face burned away in the sudden warmth. "I've slept in worse places, I promise."

I headed towards Risti's bedroom and leaned against the wall, staring blankly at the bed.

Was she right?

Was I just worried about getting hurt?

Of course I was.

But I remembered the way his body had felt beneath me as we were wrapped in the darkness in the park.

How desperate I had been for him.

How much I still wanted him.

I'd survive.

But would I survive not ever knowing what more we could have?

I glanced around the room, took in the obsessively tidy racks of enhancers and dyes, the triple-sized cleaning tube next to the wide bed.

I stopped. Wondered.

And went to check.

Somehow in the few moments she'd been gone, Risti had managed to change the sheets.

A wave of absurdity crashed over me.

"I guess we're all in agreement then," I whispered.

I took a deep breath, then another.

And walked back into the front room.

Quinn sprang to his feet from where he'd been sitting, back against the wall, facing the door. "What's wrong?"

"Nothing's wrong," I said, walking towards him, hands outstretched. "I'm just not tired."

This was it. Now or never.

"I thought maybe you could do something about

that."

He took a step towards me, paused. "Are you certain?" For the first time, he sounded unsure, questioning.

And in return, all of my fears faded away. "Positive." I closed the space between us and he swept me up in his arms.

My stomach plummeted just as it had when I fell off the seawall, but his arms were strong around me, just like they had been then.

"I'm sure Risti has all sorts of toys," I teased, my lips pressed against his neck.

"I don't want any of that," he said, long strides carrying us into the bedroom. "I only want you."

We fell on the bed in a tangle, with heated kisses and roving hands pulling at clothing, skin sliding over skin.

Everywhere his hand touched burned with electricity, my nerves were on fire.

I started to wave the lights off, but he stopped me, pinning my wrist above my head.

"No, let me see you."

And I could refuse him nothing, consumed by the heat of his gaze.

With painstaking control, he pulled my shirt over my head, and before I realized what he was doing, he wrapped it around my wrists, hooking it over the top of the bedframe.

"Stay there for a moment," he murmured, and fell upon me.

His tongue traced fiery patterns down my neck, then he darted kisses on one breast, kneading and squeezing the other with one hand.

As he nipped and licked the swollen nipple, his other hand made short work of the fastening on my pants.

"Quinn!" I shrieked as his hand cupped over my mound and reached further down, his broad fingers brushing lightly, teasingly over my slick folds.

He squeezed my breast tighter and lifted his head to grin delightedly at me.

"You have no idea what that does to me."

His fingers flicked against my clit, then slowly, carefully, he pushed one finger inside me.

I groaned and he shifted on the bed to capture my cries with his mouth.

With every thrust, he went deeper, rocking back and forth, the pressure against my aching clit almost too much to bear.

Then he pushed a second finger in and I shuddered.

But he didn't stop.

He drove harder, demanding more, until every nerve in my body stretched taut, quivering.

And finally, with one more twisting thrust, I crashed over the edge.

Quinn untangled my wrists and pulled my shaking body into his arms, crushing me to his chest while stars still spun before my eyes.

"There you are," he whispered. "I've got you, always have you." As my shaking subsided, he laid me back down on the bed, then tugged my boots off and tucked the covers around us both.

I curled drowsily on his chest as his hands stroked my back.

"Think you can sleep now?" he asked, but I was too drowsy to answer and drifted off.

I drifted, half sleeping, half remembering the day. The strange events were falling into place one after the other, tumbling down like bricks in a broken wall.

Then I sat up, wide awake again.

"I never finished telling you!" I blurted.

Quinn blinked slowly and sat up to face me. "Finished telling me what?"

"About who I thought you were at first. I mean, of course you're not, but the one who I thought you were just for that flash of moment."

"Right," he nodded. "In all the chaos, with the angry corporate boss and the attempted abduction and the bleeding, we didn't get back to that part." He pushed up to rest his back against the wall.

"So who was it?" he asked.

"Well, the thing is," I bit my lip, "I don't actually

know his name. But I know other things. He comes in about every six months, and over time, he's mentioned stuff. I know he's a trapper, lives way up in the northern wastelands. He brings in gorin pelts."

"What's a gorin? Another one of your cute little three-eyed blue things?"

"Not exactly," I shuddered. "They're flat out nasty. They're not native here, someone brought them to Heladae for sport hunting, but then all the hunters got devoured. The gorin packs moved north, started claiming territory, wiping out all the local fauna."

I wrapped the sheet around me, trying to remember more fragments. "Most people aren't bothered because they don't get anywhere near most of the settlements. If they did, I bet people would care pretty fast."

"All right," Quinn said. "How many areas do those things live in?"

"I think they've split into three or four colonies." My shoulders slumped. "It doesn't make any sense, I'm sorry. I think I was half asleep and all of a sudden, I thought I had the answer. It's like waking up from a dream, and realizing none of it made sense."

"He says he lives up in the wastelands, close enough to hunt gorin easily. And he only comes into town to refresh his supplies." Quinn sounded thoughtful. "Risti did suggest we get out of town. How warm is your coat?"

QUINN

That possible possibility I'd told Mack about was getting more likely.

Sure, it didn't have to be one of our pack brothers out there, but if there was some wild creature that nobody wanted to tangle with except for one crazy trapper?

Sounded close enough to family for me.

"Next step, how do we get up there?"

Much to my regret, Trini had pulled her shirt back on and was tucking it into her pants.

"The company that imported the gorin here went bankrupt. So of course, all of their assets, including their cruisers, were defaulted."

"To Mada Sommu," I said grimly. "Well, surely she's not using all of them."

"Look," Trini said, leading me back into the front of Risti's apartment, and pulling up a map on the wall screen. "Here's where we are, and there's the vehicle depot. I don't know for certain, but it would make sense to me that's where she stored them." She shrugged. "Unless she found a buyer for them."

"That's not too far from here." I traced over the gridlines, nodding. "If we stick to the side streets, we should be able to make it without being detected."

"And are we just going to ask Mada for the access codes?"

"Actually, I was looking forward to getting those myself."

Keeping to the shadows, we crossed the city. Trini hadn't gotten much sleep, but nerves kept her moving. I was just glad I wasn't carrying a 250- pound mountain of an ex-fighter this time.

"Here, that's the depot offices." Trini pointed to a squat, nondescript building. "I came here once with Russar when he wanted to rent a hopper to surprise Paulo with a daytrip to the country to see the sintha trees bloom. All transportation from out of Rondi comes in and out of here." She tilted her head. "Except for yours, I'm guessing. How did you get to Heladae, anyway?"

"That's a good guess, and probably not a conversation we should have right this moment," I admitted.

"How about we bring it up when we are safely on our way north?"

It took very little to convince the access port of the building that I belonged there.

When I closed the door behind us, I wiped our incursion from the log.

"What are you doing?" Trini asked.

"Just tidying as we go. It's easier than having to remember things later."

It might be true that nothing shut down in Rondi City, but certainly this late at night, they kept it to a skeleton staff.

"All we have to do is find an unoccupied office, somewhere nice and tucked away," I said as we eased down the hall. "This will do nicely."

I slid open the door and listened for anything my enhanced senses could pick up. But this section of the building was still, silent.

"Let's see what we've got in here."

Trini perched on the edge of the desk while I pulled up the records.

"Sloppy, sloppy, sloppy" I chided. "I'll have to find something better than this to take home to Nixie or she'll pout."

Trini stiffened slightly. "This Nixie," she said, her voice carefully casual. "I don't believe you've mentioned her before?"

"An obnoxious AI that eats encryption like candy," I answered distractedly, fingers flying. "And she's getting spoiled."

"Oh." Trini blinked but didn't ask anything further.

Getting into the vehicle inventory was simple.

Finding where the specially modified craft that had been designed for northern wasteland hunting trips were stored took a moment more.

"There's a massive vehicle structure beneath the building," I told Trini. "The ones we want are still there, just pretty deep down."

The entry codes were conveniently attached to the inventory.

Not just sloppy, but lazy.

We had what we'd come for, but now that I was in the system, I couldn't resist a look around.

"If they're this sloppy, what else did they leave open?" I muttered.

"I think we should go." Trini looked nervous. "If you've got the vehicle codes, we need to get out of here."

"I know," I agreed, scanning through files as quickly as I could, checking paths, looking for anything, a loose thread to pull. "But we also need to find out what's going on, and this might be our best shot."

Sliding through the network, I found what I'd hoped for.

So many of Heladae's systems were connected, so many of Mada Sommu's businesses deeply intertwined, that having access to this one poorly guarded network let me go up the chain, a virtual backdoor into her more theoretically secure databases.

And now I was in.

I flicked through directories as fast as I could, searching for something, anything that might help us.

Jackpot

One massive folder, nearly bursting at the digital seams.

SEC_LOGS

Security Logs.

Thousands of files, stretching so far back that either someone had forgotten to purge them, or it was Mada's policy to save them forever for record keeping or blackmail material.

Probably the same thing, as far as she was concerned.

"We don't have time to go through so many," Trini gasped as the list of files spooled across the screen.

"Something changed today, maybe yesterday, right?" I asked.

And that narrowed it down, but not enough.

I tapped my fingers on the desk, thinking.

Trini kept scrolling through. "Are all conversations everywhere in town logged?

"I doubt it," I answered distractedly. "Everywhere in town would require massive data storage. No, just looks like she keeps audio files for all of her buildings."

"You mean, like this one?" Trini asked with a raised eyebrow.

Void!

Quickly I checked for bugs.

Nothing.

"I should have thought of that first. Thanks."

"No worries," she said, the tightness of her voice betraying the words. "I'm getting good at being paranoid."

I flipped through a dozen of the recordings on high speed, volume set so low I could barely hear it.

Another dozen. Nothing of interest

"Quinn..."

"I know, I know. Just a few more, then I'll give it up."

There we go.

I turned the volume up slightly. "That's Mada's voice, right?"

Trini nodded. "But she's talking about increasing rent for some of the booths in the Carnival. That's nothing to do with us."

"Nope, but that'll make the next step easier."

Quickly I bashed out a voiceprint match, set the date for the last three days, and waited for it to filter.

Started listening to the stack of files it flagged.

Normal business. Normal business, with a very cutthroat margin.

Then something that didn't seem to be business as usual at all.

"I'll kill the bastard," Mada snarled.

I glanced up at Trini.

"Oh yeah, that's her," she confirmed, eyes wide.

A second voice cut in, one we didn't recognize, but I'd remember. *"The access logs are clear, ma'am. He's the only one who's accessed those files. We found the comm he downloaded them on, but the interface has been wiped. He must have copied the files somewhere else."*

"Who would have thought pretty little Makkar had the brains to try something like this," Mada mused.

"We've searched his quarters, ma'am. There's nothing of interest there. What are your orders?"

"He's stupid, but not so stupid to keep the files on him," she answered. *"Follow everywhere he goes. He's made a drop somewhere. Stashed it or already sold it."*

"What do you think he's planning?"

"I'd bet he's looking for a buyer, someone off-world, someone from one of the other corps," Mada said. *"I could make a list of people who would love to buy what he's selling, but it wouldn't do us any good at this point."*

"Could he try to use the files against you directly, sell them back to you?" the second voice asked.

Even without video, you could hear the deadly smile in her voice. *"I'd like to see him try."*

Then the audio ended.

"They must have gone outside, or entered another section of the building. Maybe there's more..."

"No," Trini insisted. "That's enough for now."

I kept searching.

"Please."

I sighed. She was right.

After clearing all traces from the access log of the terminal, we slipped out of the room as quietly as we'd come in.

Still smarting at my carelessness, I checked for bugs as we went deeper inside the building.

Nothing, but as we reached the elevator that led to the vehicle structure, we stayed silent.

Level 120 46-A was a long ride down, and the car jolted slightly as it changed direction, moving laterally to deliver us to the right area.

As we stepped out of the elevator, an automatic light flickered on and I swore under my breath.

"Nothing to do about it now," I muttered. "I'll erase it before we leave." This was getting annoying.

Then we found the vehicle, and all other smaller concerns were swept away.

"It's huge," Trini breathed. "And," she squinted at it, tilting her head, "is it shimmering?"

"Passive optical camouflage system," I guessed. "Unfortunately, these don't come in a more reasonable size."

I'd checked. Because I'd really rather not be trying to sneak around in something the size of a small building.

But there wasn't a choice. None of the other vehicles, either owned by Mada, her companies, or those belonging to visitors, were equipped to travel the northern wastes.

If I ignored the camouflage, it was still an ugly thing. Blocky and matte gray, the prow was shaped like a blunt wedge. Two stories high, it sat on eight bulky tires that would fold up and tuck into the undercarriage when it shifted to hover mode.

The ships had never been fully decommissioned, sitting here stocked and fueled, waiting for visitors that never came.

Until us.

"How are we going to hide the fact that we took this thing?" Trini wondered.

"They won't know it's missing unless someone who knows how many there should be actually comes down here to count them," I answered. "I altered the inventory, made it look like there's only been three of these things."

"That's a start," she nodded. "I guess we'd better get going."

Sending the access code to the onboard receiver, a thick door swung open and a ramp lowered. "That's handy at least," Trini said as she started up.

My nerves bristled, walking behind her. I'd already checked that the vehicle was empty before we came down. No one should have seen us, known we were here, what we were looking for.

And still, it was hard to keep from pushing her behind me, standing between her and the unknown.

Except she'd probably be pissed. That was enough to make me stop.

This time.

From the entry deck, a short flight of steps led down to the left and the cockpit. Another set spiraled up to the right, presumably to the living quarters.

"Let's get out of here, then we can check the rest of it out together, alright?" I proposed.

Trini didn't argue, just followed me into the cockpit. "Any idea how to work one of these things?" she asked, looking at the console that stretched across the front.

"It can't be too difficult," I decided. "Not if they were renting them out."

After a brief study, most of it seemed clear enough. "There's a preprogrammed flight path to go to the planned hunting ground," I announce. "We can figure out the rest of the controls on the way, but until we're well out of the city, I'll need you to monitor the screens, okay?"

"This doesn't seem the best time for me to train to be a pilot," she squeaked. "I've never even wanted to learn."

"Relax," I said, as I pull my personal commtab out from my bag, interfaced it with the local network, and started working. "You've got good hand-eye coordination, you'll be a natural. And right now, I don't even need you to steer. Let the ship do its own thing, and let me know if anything starts flashing. Or turns red." I thought for a moment. "Maybe alarms would be a good thing, too."

The vehicle hummed as it powered on and sealed up, only the slightest vibration when it rose fractionally into the air, wheels turning underneath.

"What are you going to be doing?" Trini asked, eying the screens warily.

"Closing the door behind us," I answered, settling back into the plush chair and focusing. Pulling up screens all around me, I found the schematic of the structure. A long ramp spiraled around the outer ring, then curved off to lead to an exit far away from the city.

"Can't have any pesky overhead traffic distracting anyone from the party," I muttered. The entire path was lined with cameras and sensors. Necessary to get us out safely.

A pain in the ass in every security sense.

One by one, as we passed each check point, I dove into the system, erasing all tracks of our progress as we went.

Not a hard task, but fiddly, taking all of my concentration.

From time to time, Trini let out a muffled gasp as the cruiser continued its journey towards the surface, but she didn't call for me, and I kept my attention on the task at hand.

Finally, I waved the screens away and looked around.

"Thank goodness," Trini said as we emerged into the predawn light. "I thought we'd never get out of there."

I rubbed my eyes, wishing I'd brought a blocker, just to ease the headache. "We should reach the edge of the wasteland by nightfall. We should get some rest, then get started narrowing down the search parameters."

"Should we check out the rest of the cruiser? See if there's a place to sleep?" she asked.

"I'm sure there is. But it might be just bunk beds. We'll have to get creative."

She blushed and stuck her tongue out. "You can get creative all you want. I'm planning on being solidly out as soon as I find anything that looks like a pillow."

She was probably right, but as she headed up the

stairs into the living quarters ahead of me, the rocking swell of her hips made me reconsider my priorities.

"They really planned to be roughing it on those hunting trips, didn't they?" Trini said as we passed through a lounge with low, comfortable-looking armchairs clustered around polished tables. Privacy screens dimmed the windows but we could still see the rolling violet hills flying by outside. A top-of-the-line replicator separated the lounge from the sleeping quarters.

They weren't bunk beds, not by a long shot.

I checked out each of the four rooms, but when I returned to the first one, Trini had already thrown herself face-down on the soft mattress, fully clothed.

"Come on, hon," I coaxed her. "Let's at least get the boots off."

As I lay in the darkened room next to her, I thought about the audio file.

Makkar had stolen something from Mada. Something she wanted back at any price.

Trini made a tiny whimper and snuggled into my shoulder. Even as I wrapped my arm around her to draw her closer, I had to wonder.

Did Trini really not know anything about Makkar's plans?

TRINI

I woke, my head groggy, confused.

The low hum surrounding me confirmed the impossible.

I was headed north, to the wastelands, trying to hunt down a mysterious trapper who may or may not be the person Quinn was looking for, and on the run from the virtual boss of the planet, who's goons had nearly killed my own boss while trying to abduct me.

I ran over it again.

Yeah, that kind of summed it up.

I opened my eyes and realized Quinn wasn't in bed anymore.

Well, it didn't really sum him up, did it?

What was I even doing here?

I thought again about that recording that Quinn had found.

He's looking for a buyer, someone off-world, someone from one of the other corps.

Russar had warned me not to trust Quinn.

But I had anyway.

Had Russar paid the price?

I shook my head and forced myself to sit up and reluctantly get out of bed.

I might have sneered a little bit at the fancy 'hunting vehicle' that the tourists had signed up to use, but I had to admit, that mattress was remarkably comfortable.

Stripping down, I tossed my clothes in the bin to be re-sterilized and stepped into the refresher.

"Temperature up," I yelped as ice cold streams filled the tube.

Slowly, the heat warmed up enough to spread through my body, helping me relax as I washed my hair and thought.

I didn't know anything about Quinn. Nothing solid.

Everything was a mystery, from the way he moved and his hacking skills, to how he had gotten here.

He was keeping secrets from me.

And I couldn't tell if I should take it personally, or if it was just how he was.

The warm air flew around me and I ran my fingers through my hair as it dried.

What did that mean for us?

Even if he had nothing to do with this whole mess with Makkar and Mada, did I want to be involved with someone who kept secrets as easily as he breathed?

I stepped out and pulled on my freshly cleaned clothes.

Leaving the boots off, I pattered down the hall to the lounge.

Quinn was there, a steaming cup of kaf in front of him.

He looked up and grinned. "I was wondering when you'd get up, but I wanted to let you sleep. It's been a busy day and you needed the rest."

I poked at the machine and got myself a cup of kaf.

"I know they won't be as good as those empies," Quinn said, "but shouldn't you have something more than that?"

I shook my head, drinking in the warm caffeinated goodness.

"Not so soon after waking up," I explained. "That's the kaf's time."

"I see." He didn't look convinced, but didn't argue. Always a plus in the mornings. Or afternoon, whatever time this was.

"I found something interesting here." He threw the screen he'd been working with up onto the wall so I could see it.

"Here are the four clusters of gorin that the satellites have picked up. We're about an hour away from this one." He pointed to a red blotch on the map.

I tapped the viewscreen and looked into the swirling white storm around us. "I don't think the coat I brought is going to be up to this."

"No worries. They've got fully insulated suits tucked away in the drawers down there." He pointed. "The replicators on that side of the aisle are programmed for boots and extra clothing if needed."

"An hour away, right?" I stood up and headed toward the replicator again. "Time for more kaf then, if we're going out in that weather."

After we suited up in thin, insulated overalls, I pulled the boots on.

"A little bit big, but not bad." I glanced around to see Quinn standing in front of another recessed cabinet. "What have you found?

"The weapons cache."

I walked behind him to take a peek. Rack upon rack of all types of blasters, long ones and short ones, and some strange, heavy-barreled ones that looked like they could take down a spaceship in flight.

"They almost look like the rifles you would find at the carnival booths." I reached out to touch one of the big blasters, then snatched my hand away. "I don't like them."

"Plasma blasters," Quinn said. "Not my favorite either, but if those creatures are as deadly as you say, we'll both be carrying them." He picked the smallest one, checked it over professionally. "This shouldn't kick too much. As soon as we get to the edge of the gorin's range we'll stop, give you some training. It won't be enough, but it'll have to do."

I wasn't looking forward to any of it, but he was right.

When the doors slid open and the ramp unfurled, the bitter shock of the frigid air took my breath away, despite the hood, facemask, and goggles.

"Your friend can't live out here, monsters or not," I insisted. "Nobody could."

"Wait for a moment," Quinn said. "Let me go out, check over the area."

"Not really in a hurry," I muttered as he disappeared into the white swirl. I stayed by the door until he returned from his circuit of the cruiser.

He checked the scanner in his hand. "I'm not reading any human science. But there's a lot of magnetic interference here. I don't think we should rely on the scanner." He waved me out. "Come on, let's get you a little more comfortable with that thing."

An hour later, I never wanted to see a blaster pistol again. "This is the one you said wouldn't have much kick?" My hand felt tingly. At least it felt something. I'm not sure my nose would ever feel anything again.

"But you're doing a great job decimating the snowman army," Quinn praised.

That was true. Once I got the hang of it, learned how gently I needed to pull the trigger, it was easier than throwing darts.

And this time there wasn't a sneaky barrier field deflecting my shots.

"What do I win?"

"Will you be happy if I say I'll go get you another one of those absurd toys?"

"I'll be happier when we go inside and I have more kaf."

He motioned for me to head up the ramp before him. "That sounds reasonable."

We went deeper into the gorin territory, but every time Quinn went outside to take scanner readings, he found nothing.

"All right," he finally said. "Let's move on to the next one."

According to the satellite data, the second pack had taken up residence not far away.

Quinn frowned at the map as the cruiser lumbered along. We had shifted it to crawler mode. The trade in energy from moving more slowly was more than made up by having a little extra heat.

"I wonder if this was an old reading," I said, tapping the first area the gorin were supposed to be living in. "From everything I've heard about them, it seemed odd that two packs of lethal apex predators would be so close to each other."

Quinn nodded thoughtfully. "You might be right, which means we need to be even more on our guard at the next stop." He scratched at the back of his head. "Something's out there. I can feel it."

This time, when Quinn brought out the scanner halfway down the ramp, even looking over his shoulder from where I'd been stationed in the doorway, I could see something was giving a reading.

"Is it your friend?" I asked, hoping we could find this guy and get back to where it was warm.

And where people want to kidnap you, I reminded myself.

"No," he shook his head. "I don't think so. This is weird." He waved at the screen and I came down the ramp a little further to get a better look. "The readings flicker, almost like something is jumping in and out of range."

"That can't be right, can it?"

"It shouldn't be right," he said. He smacked the device with the flat of his hand, but nothing changed. "Hardware isn't exactly my specialty. But no life signs should be able to jump in and out of the range of this thing like that."

The screen seemed to be a jumble of spots, dots of red winking in and out all around us.

"What if it's picking up something else entirely?" I asked. "Or what if the gorin have something like the cruiser's camouflage? You said that should keep us from being picked up by satellite?"

I didn't need to see his face under the mask to imagine his expression. "Wouldn't that be perfect. Vicious beasts that are too dangerous to hunt, that can't even be tracked. It would be like—"

But I didn't hear the rest of what he was saying because I'd been flung from the ramp into the snow.

The impact knocked the breath out of me, my shoulder felt crushed, my chest cramped, tight.

Then I realized it wasn't just that I wasn't breathing, something had a hold of me.

I thrashed, hoping to clear my vision, to get away, but an otherworldly howl covered my screams.

And then Quinn was there.

With a roar, he grabbed the beast, holding it over his head before throwing it back into the swirling snow.

"Quinn!" I shouted as another massive form barreled out of the whiteness.

It was a thing of nightmares, barely visible against

the storm, hulking thick body and long arms covered with thick white fur.

Six eyes scattered over its head tracked every move we made, and long yellowed fangs were bared for the attack.

Just in time, Quinn spun, blunting the creature's impact, but still it tossed him aside, then sprang over me towards him.

I scrambled up, shoulder throbbing from where I'd hit the ground.

I had to do something, had to help, somehow, anyhow.

The creature leaped at Quinn again, pinning him to the ground, but with a twist and a kick, he sent it flying.

"Get back into the cruiser!" he shouted at me.

I struggled to my feet and nearly fell again.

Sharp knives of pain shot up my leg as I put my weight on my left ankle.

He was right.

I had to get out of the way.

Exposed, I was nothing more than a distraction for Quinn.

Potentially a fatal one.

The first gorin had scuttled back, the two now circling around Quinn, watching, waiting for an opening.

Slowly, I crawled back towards the ramp, trying not to look at the battle.

Watching wouldn't help him.

A little more, ignoring the growls and thuds behind me.

Closer I crept, then a glint of metal in the snow caught my eye.

Quinn's plasma rifle.

Easily three times the length of the pistol I had practiced with, it lay half buried in the snow from when he'd been tackled by the second gorin.

I dragged myself to it, grabbed it, and turned so I sat splay-legged in the snow, my legs slowly growing numb despite the insulated suit.

The gorin took turns leaping and snarling at Quinn, driving him further away from me.

He dodged, kicked, and struck.

But I knew he couldn't do that forever.

Eventually he would tire.

And they would tear him apart.

I raised the rifle, sighted it, and shaking, lowered it back down.

What was I thinking?

An hour's practice with the pistol and I thought I could make a target from here?

I'd be just as likely to shoot Quinn.

The gorin screamed as they attacked again and this

time, Quinn's arm snapped out, snagging one out of the air mid-jump.

In a flash, he straddled its back, wrenching the massive jaws open, wider and wider until finally, he ripped the lower jaw off.

Ripped the lower jaw off and used it to batter at the creature's eyes.

But while he was focused on the one, the other had circled behind him.

I raised the rifle again, settled it against my shoulder,

and fired.

Both Quinn and the monster froze, but Quinn recovered faster, jumping from the first monster's back and attacking the second, raining fists down upon its head until, with a sickening crack, the skull crunched open.

I fell back in the snow, half-stunned from the recoil.

Thankfully, my warning shot had gone as wide as I'd hoped but still done its job, distracting the monster enough for Quinn to have a chance.

The two carcasses lay still in the snow when Quinn slowly raised himself to his feet.

He staggered to me, slung the rifle over his shoulder, and swept me up in his arms. "Come on," he said. "Let's get out of here."

Up the ramp he carried me, but then I cried out. "Stop!"

"Not until you're inside," he growled.

"But we need that," I insisted, pointing over his shoulder to where the scanner sat abandoned in the snow.

Quinn grunted, placed me carefully on the steps leading up to the living quarters and leaped into the snow to retrieve the device.

I'd barely had time to pull my goggles off when he was back inside, sealing us in.

"Shouldn't we keep moving, check out the next location?" I asked, as he put the scanner and the rifle carefully down in the cockpit and turned back to me.

His goggles were cracked and his suit was splattered with the gorin's blood. But still, when he reached for me, I didn't shrink back.

"I just need a minute to make sure you're alright first," he said, his low voice slightly unsteady.

"I'm fine," I said in disbelief, realizing not all of the blood was from the gorin. Three parallel gashes opened up his side. "But we've got to get you taken care of. Those claws..." I shuddered. "There's got to be something here that will keep you from getting infected with whatever nastiness those things carry."

He lifted me back into his arms and we headed back

through the lounge towards the bedroom. "Let's start with getting cleaned up and go from there."

When he put me down, I winced and wobbled, frantically clutching at his shoulders for balance.

"What happened?" he demanded. "Did you break anything?"

Without waiting for an answer, he tore the rest of the suit off me, shredding it at the boot tops and tossing it into the recycler without a second look.

He ran his hands carefully over my body, the fierce look of concentration almost comical as I blushed, stripped to my underwear and boots before him.

"I'm fine," I insisted, cupping one hand over his check, forcing his head up so that I could pull the goggles off his face and make him meet my eyes. "My shoulder's a little banged up, and I twisted my ankle when I fell. That's all."

His eyes narrowed, but since he couldn't find any other wounds on me, he eventually nodded. "We can fix that." Helping me to the edge of the bed, he disappeared down the hall again.

In a moment, he was back, a slim black rod in his hand. "Let's get that boot off." He knelt down beside the bed, pulled off the boot from my uninjured foot, and slowly unfastened the side seal of the other. I could already feel it swelling. "This isn't going to be fun. I'm sorry."

"Wait, what?"

But before the words had left my lips, he'd whipped the boot off in one smooth motion.

"Ouch!" I yipped.

"I know, sweetheart, I know," he soothed, then started running the rod back and forth over my ankle, an inch from my skin. Soothing warmth penetrated the joint and the jagged throbbing faded into a dull ache.

He kept working over my ankle, but all I could see was the wound on his side.

If words weren't going to convince him, it was time for a more direct approach.

"That's enough, into the cleaner." I stood up gingerly, but the wand had done its work.

I stepped away from him, towards the refresher, and slowly, teasingly, pulled my panties off.

Careful this time to set the water temperature higher first, I stepped into the jets.

"Aren't you going to join me?"

QUINN

Maybe the claws on those things did have some sort of paralyzing agent on them.

I stood, mind frozen, as the steam fogged up the refresher tube so that all I could see was glimpses of Trini's perfect body.

Her all too fragile body.

When the creature had attacked her, I thought I'd lose my mind.

At that moment, I realized I didn't care if she had stolen whatever data Mada had lost, if she'd somehow been caught up in a plot with Makkar.

I only cared that she was safe.

And mine.

I moved towards the refresher door, then checked myself.

Her suit had probably been salvageable, before I tore it off her.

Mine, well, not so much.

As quickly as I'd stripped her, I pulled the tattered thing off me, wincing a little when I twisted against the gashes. That was going to sting for a few hours.

I opened the door and slid in behind her, running my hands down her back to the sweet dimples right above her ass.

"I was beginning to wonder if you were ever going to get here," she teased.

She turned to face me, wrapping her arms around my neck. "This isn't quite as big as the one in Risti's apartment, so we'll have to get friendly."

"I don't see a problem with that," I said, stooping towards her, but she dodged to the side.

"First you need to get rinsed off."

"I'll be fine," I grumbled, but she was right. Those things had been filthy. I could still smell the creatures' rancid, reeking breath.

I hissed as the hot water sluiced through the gashes, and Trini bit her lip.

"They're not as deep as they look. When we're out, you can take the wand to them, but I promise, they'll be all healed up by morning," I tried to reassure her, but the wrinkles didn't smooth from her forehead.

"Do you need a painkiller?" she asked, reaching for

the door. "I'll bet there's something wherever you found that healing wand."

"I have something else in mind that'll make the pain go away," I said, and this time when I pulled her close, I didn't let her wiggle away.

She squirmed against me until I rocked my hips, nudging her belly with my hard length. "You're not exactly distracting me."

For a moment, her hazel eyes lost focus as her mouth opened into a sweet, soft 'oh'. The tiny pink triangle of her tongue flicked out and back again, and my gut felt like I'd been struck by a hammer.

I bent over to breathe in the scent of her arousal, dizzy with need for her. "Tell me no, quickly," I begged, feeling my control slip by the second.

Then I froze at the burning touch of her hands wrapped around my cock.

"Yes," she breathed.

Groaning, I fell to my knees in front of her, slipping my hands between her knees to open her legs, wrapping around to the back of her thighs.

She stumbled forward, hands on my shoulders, laughing as I dotted kisses down her belly, then gasped as I lifted her to sit splayed open for me, her slight weight resting on my forearms.

I dragged my tongue hungrily over her wet folds, her soft cries spurring me on. My fingers dug into the lush curves of her hips as I stood, carrying her with me.

I broke away long enough to order the water off, then kicked the door open.

Laying her down on the bed, I devoured her with my gaze, her every dewy curve, the rise and fall of her chest as she panted, her eyes dilated and wondering.

I slid next to her, skimming my hand down her side, unable to stop touching her, tasting her.

"You've done something to me," I murmured, lips pressed against her neck, ranging over her soft skin to nibble at the shell of her ear. "I have a job to do, a mission. But all I want is you."

Trini rolled towards me, her hand sliding around my back, pulling me towards her. "Lucky for you, I'm right here," she whispered.

I rolled on top of her, elbows pinning her arms to her sides, hands curled over her shoulders from beneath.

"Next time I'll be gentle, I promise." I moved, just slightly, just enough to nudge the head of my cock against her silken folds. "Next time we'll go slow. This time, I don't know if I can."

In response, she wrapped her legs around my waist, curving her pelvis up slightly. "I never asked for gentle or slow," she said, and nipped at my neck with her sharp little teeth. "I'm not as fragile as you think."

The feel of her under me, her legs around me, her fingernails digging into my back, all twisted together to push me towards the edge.

I eased into her, fighting for control, but then she bit me again, and growling, I drove forward, one hard thrust until I was fully seated within her.

Her eyelids fluttered shut. "Quinn," she moaned.

I fought to see her clearly through the haze in my mind. "Are you all right?" I croaked.

"Do that again," she ordered, and I'd never been so happy to obey a command in my life.

Afterwards, we lay panting, tangled in the damp sheets.

"We really should have dried off first," she murmured sleepily, burrowing closer against my shoulder.

"There's an easy fix for that," I said, then gently eased her into my arms and carried her to the next bedroom down the hall.

"Are we just going to move rooms every night?" Trini snuggled down into the pillow. I pulled the cover up over her shoulders and brushed her still damp hair back from her face.

"We'll run out of rooms eventually," I answered, even though I doubted she could hear me. "But sure, why not?"

Returning to our original room, I pulled a pair of

pants from my bag, grabbed my commtab, and padded out to the cockpit.

For a while now, I'd been hearing a rhythmic thumping from outside, even when I was too distracted to do anything about it.

And now on the cruiser's sensors, I could see them.

A pack of gorin throwing themselves futilely at the ship's hull.

"You're not getting in, no matter how much you knock," I muttered, and searched through the console to see if there was a way to electrify the hull.

Didn't find one. Pity.

I stowed the rifle back into the weapons rack and set the cruiser's autopilot to take us to the next area to investigate.

I flipped open a channel to Mack, still waiting above in the *Queen*.

After a second, the line hissed. "Keep your voice down, Zayda's sleeping."

The *Queen* was small enough that there was no privacy, but I pitched my voice low enough that if Zayda was back in one of the sleeping bunks, Mack would have no trouble hearing me without the risk of waking her.

"Sorry. Haven't had much of a chance to check in until now," I offered.

"You've been silent for too long," he snarled. "Zayda was getting worried."

I laughed softly. Mack might never admit to being concerned about any members of the family he still only half remembered, but an inconvenience to his mate was to be treated as a grave insult.

"Tell her I'm sorry. The local situation is getting complicated."

"You told me last time there'd been an attack on a girl. Do we need to worry about it?"

I bristled. "Of course we need to worry about it," I snarled. "They scared her, could have hurt her."

Mack was silent for a long minute. "I thought you said it was local politics, that we shouldn't get involved."

"We're involved," I answered shortly. "That thin lead is panning out," I said after I got myself back under control. "There's a hunter, a trapper, something like that, up in the north wilds making a living killing off monsters. Tangled with two of the damned things earlier tonight myself. Can't imagine anyone other than one of us deciding it was a smart way to live."

What kind of monsters? Nixie asked. *Do they have wings? Do they have tentacles? Would Vicki like one for a pet?*

"No!" Mack and I both declared.

"I'll send you specs to look at, but don't give them to

Doc," I ordered. "She doesn't need any more bright ideas. And no, Vicki can't have one for a pet. And Eris doesn't need one to help with the baby."

Did that cover everything?

With Nixie, you could only do your best and hope.

"Are you sure you don't need a hand?" Mack asked. "It's boring as hell up here. Not sure why you should get all the fun."

"Let's see how this plays out," I said. "If Torik is out here, I want to find out why before we get too many of us tangled up in this."

"Not much to tangle. Go down, pick him up, get out."

"Except," I said slowly, "I want to know what he's been doing here this whole time. Why didn't he come home when the rest of us did?"

Silence, broken by the crackle of static.

"Yeah, that's a good question," Mack admitted. "Let me know if you need some help getting an answer. I'll leave you to play your hand as you want. Just don't forget you've got backup."

"Yeah. Now I've got to get some sleep."

I cut the connection and scratched at my side. Healing always itched terribly, felt like the nerves were on fire while the tissue rebuilt itself.

I ran a hand over where the wound had been.

Almost gone. Good. Trini probably would be fussy about getting the sheets bloody.

I checked the map.

The cruiser had left the gorin pack in its metaphorical dust while I'd been catching up with Mack, but it would still be hours before we were at the next possible site.

I yawned, stretching.

A solid night's sleep would finish up the healing process.

Besides, I wasn't going to turn down an opportunity to curl up next to my mate.

IN THE MORNING, I woke to find Trini peering at me from those enormous hazel eyes.

"What are you looking at?" I asked.

"I've never gotten a chance to just watch you," she said, and a flash of panic ran through me.

"You're always moving, leaping into action, concentrated on your screens," she continued. "I don't think I've ever just seen you still before."

I sat up and ran my fingers through my hair, then rubbed my eyes with the heel of my palm.

"I don't usually sleep a lot," I admitted. "Always seems like there's too much to do."

"Quinn!" she gasped. "Your side! It's almost like it never happened."

She ran her fingers over my ribs, until I took her hand in my own and kissed the inside of her wrist.

"You keep doing that, and there's going to be a delay before you get your kaf."

She wiggled past me to get out of bed, carefully testing her weight on her ankle. She flipped through the replicator until she found the screen for a silky soft robe. "Did you use the healing wand after I went to sleep? I'm so glad it did such a good job. I think I'm going to need another round before I try to get back into boots."

Guilt kicked my gut. "Yeah, the wand did better than expected."

Pulling the robe on, she headed to the lounge area. "Come on, sleepyhead. I want to see where we are."

I waited until she'd had her first cup of kaf before breaking the news. "You're not going back out there."

"Excuse me?" She put the mug down with exaggerated slowness. "Repeat that?"

"Trini." I reached for her hand, but she pulled it back. "Those things could have killed me, killed you."

"And you think I'm just a distraction," she said bitterly.

"No, I mean, yes, I'm always distracted while you're around," I admitted. Her slight grin was a partial reward. "But you've barely had any training with the plasma weapons. If I can't defeat one of those things, how much damage do you expect to do?"

"Then you're out there alone," she said, "with no one to watch your back."

I thought of Mack's offer. But no matter how much he meant it, he'd worry about Zayda, lethal competent ex-spy that she was.

She and Trini would get along, I thought, then quickly swept the idea away.

"Look, let's get suited up, and you stay by the door," I offered. "Watch the sensors, watch the landscape. I could use another set of eyes."

She scowled, silent. I went to the replicator. "Do you think this thing can make cones? Maybe not as good as the ones in that shop, but maybe something close. Maybe even with sprinkles."

"I'm not that easily distracted," she grumbled.

"Never thought you were, just thought maybe I hadn't given them enough of a chance."

From behind, she wrapped her arms around my waist, pressing her cheek into my back. "Don't you think we have enough frozen weather outside?"

And I knew that she might not be happy with my solution, but she'd forgiven me.

A little bit.

After we suited up, I checked the sensor as we stood

by the door. Trini perched at the opening, a long-barreled rifle in her lap.

I'd taken the heaviest of the guns. Sure, I could try to keep beating the gorin in hand-to-hand combat, but it'd be a hell of a lot easier to just take it down with one shot.

Less risk to me, or to Trini.

Just as it had yesterday, the scanner gave the same jumbled reading, red dots flickering in and out.

"I'm going to go out, see if I can get anything clearer," I said, and kissed the top of her hooded head before pulling up my own facemask and tightening my goggles.

"Remember, do just like you did before. If you see anything, fire off a warning shot. I'll be back here on the double."

I circled the cruiser but found nothing except more swirling snow.

No tracks, no life signs.

Nothing.

I waved to Trini as I reached the bottom of the ramp again.

"I'm going to go out a little bit farther" I called up to her. "Make another loop."

She gave an awkward thumbs up, hand bundled in the insulated glove.

The drifts were deeper farther out. A few old tracks, mostly buried in snow.

But still, nothing. No sign of Torik.

As I circled back to the ramp, I looked up at Trini.

But she was gone, her rifle abandoned on the floor, unfired.

TRINI

I hated to admit it, but Quinn had been right.

Even just sitting, sheltered by the edge of the cruiser's door, the icy wind seemed to find even the slightest opening in my suit.

I stared out again into the blinding landscape, chewing on my lip beneath my mask.

Maybe I hadn't noticed before, but the weather, if possible, was getting worse. What had been a constant steady fall of snow was turning into a full-out blizzard.

What an awful place.

So far, the only signs of life had been the gorin. What did they even eat up here?

I shivered, this time not only because of the cold.

Not us.

Right now, keeping us off the menu was all that mattered.

I stared out, half dreading seeing any movement, until I had to close my eyes to rest them from the overwhelming whiteness, despite the polarized lenses of the goggles.

A whisper of sound, more the feel of the air moving around me, and I snapped my eyes open again.

A gorin crouched next to me in the doorway.

I raised the rifle, but it smacked it out of my hand and lunged towards me, knocking the breath out of me before I could scream.

I shook my head to clear it, then realized I was already upside down over its shoulder as it bounded away into the thickening blizzard.

"Quinn!" I shouted and beat on its back with my fists. "Put me down!" I screamed again, but then it shifted me, pulled me to its front and covered my mouth, never once slowing its loping run.

My mind stuttered, pieces shifting into a new picture.

That was a gloved hand over my mouth, not a clawed paw.

It was running upright, not on all fours.

It wasn't a gorin at all.

And that didn't make me feel one bit better.

I thrashed harder, struggling to break free, but the strong arm around me didn't ease up in the slightest.

Finally, I stopped kicking and started thinking.

What would I do even if I did get free?

I forced myself to relax, trying to take even breaths and clear my mind.

My attacker had already left the cruiser far behind.

If I managed to get away, would I just wander, lost and alone in the snow, trying to find my way back to Quinn?

Would I even survive long enough to find him?

No, if this was another human, maybe this was the man Quinn was looking for.

Either way, he had to have some sort of shelter that he was taking me to. No one could survive out here unprotected.

It seemed like hours passed, but I had no way to tell time. The landscape never varied, just glimpses of monotonous white.

Finally, the man's steps angled slightly and I craned my head, only to recoil back against his chest.

A vast wall of ice cut across the landscape before us.

And we weren't slowing down.

Suddenly, everything was dark and I realized we'd entered a narrow crack, a crevice in the ice-covered rock wall.

I tried to pull myself into a small ball, but I couldn't break free.

My captor twisted and turned, following the tunnel until finally he stepped out into a well-lit cave.

To my surprise, once we reached the middle of the cavern, the man dropped me as if surprised he had carried me so far.

I scrambled back away from him. "Who are you? Why did you bring me here?" I demanded, trying to keep my voice even, but not succeeding very well.

He didn't answer, just turned his back on me, pulled off the layers of gorin skin that made up his coat, and went to tend the fire.

When the light struck his face, I realized it was true.

This was the man that came every few months to the Merry Stormcloud, the one that I'd mistaken Quinn for.

But he didn't seem to recognize me at all.

I took a moment to study him, just as I had this morning while Quinn was sleeping.

What was it that had made them seem so similar?

Standing by the fire, he pulled off another layer until he was down to a thin long-sleeved shirt.

I looked away. A month ago, I would have kept watching. But now, when I wasn't sure what lay between Quinn and me, it just seemed wrong, uncomfortable.

I'd certainly seen enough to know that they were both strongly muscled, powerful men. The way he'd moved through the snow, twisting through the cleft in the rock to reach this cave, was amazing, uncanny.

Quinn moved like that, when he'd caught me at the seawall, when he'd fought off the attackers in my room, and against the gorin.

But there was something more. I'd noticed it while Quinn slept just this morning, which seemed like days and days ago now.

The tips of his ears were pointed. Just a bit.

Not enough to make a statement, to be obvious. Which made me suspect it wasn't from one of the popular cosmetic modifications.

If you were going to spend the money for something like that, surely you'd have the work be more noticeable, exaggerated, even.

You could barely see the shape of Quinn's ears through his thick hair.

But enough for a lover to notice, gazing at him as he slept, running fingers lightly over his features.

And now that I knew what to look for, I saw this man had those same strange ears as well, even if his hair was darker, shaggier.

If it wasn't a cosmetic enhancement, if their speed and strength weren't the standard set of buffing modifications that most mercs spent half their pay on, then what were we talking about?

Something else.

Something secret.

I approached the fire cautiously, but the man didn't chase me away. I took the mask and goggles off, then pushed my hair back so he could see me.

"Remember me? I see you when you come into town, to the bar. You always order two korvasian brandies, neat."

I took another step closer. "I'm not usually dressed in all of this," I said, waving down at the suit. "You sit in the back, away from the stage. You told me once you were a hunter, right?"

Slowly, recognition donned in his eyes. "You're a long way from Rondi City."

Something else they had in common. Their voices sounded like a growl, even in normal tones. I wondered if his voice dropped to an inhumanly low pitch, like Quinn's had.

I bet it did.

I took yet another step towards the fire, craving the warmth. "Do you mind?"

"Of course not." He looked around, frowning, as if trying to remember where we were, and why.

Not entirely reassuring.

"I'm curious, if you don't mind me asking." I

crouched down by the fire, half wondering what he'd found to burn up in this bleak land. "Do you make it a habit to kidnap anybody you find up here?"

I thought about those missing hunters.

Was that due to the monsters, or did this guy have something to do with it?

He scoffed. "It'd bring more trouble than it's worth, bringing them back here."

That didn't exactly answer the question, but maybe I didn't want to know any more.

"Then why did you grab me?" I wondered.

"Because I wanted a word with your companion," he said. "Maybe."

I shook my head, exasperated. "You could've just said hello. I think he's been looking for you, too."

"Not out there," he said. "Too open, too easy to get distracted, get attacked."

"That's all well and good," I snapped, not sure he was making any sense at all, and becoming slowly convinced I was trapped with a madman. "But how do you expect him to find you in the middle of a snowstorm?"

"If he finds me, that answers one question. If he doesn't," he shrugged. "I'll take you back into town myself."

"This is crazy!" There wasn't a way to reach someone who seemed to be having a different conversation than the one I was having. "Everything about this is insane," I muttered.

Then Quinn came charging through the crevice, and insane took on a whole new meaning.

Almost before I could register his presence, he leaped over the fire, hands twisted into claws to wrap around the stranger's throat.

But the dark-haired man twisted, grabbed Quinn's arm, and smacked it back.

The two of them fought silently, fists and feet flying too fast to see, rolling and punching back and forth across the cave floor.

I stood still, in shock.

This was somehow worse than when Quinn had fought the gorin.

They'd been savage, but here, Quinn's fluid fighting style was mirrored back at him, every brutal blow reflected by his opponent.

And they showed no signs of slowing down.

"Quinn, stop it! I'm alright!" I shouted.

But my words didn't get through to him.

I looked around frantically, hoping to find something I could use to distract them, a way to fire a warning shot, anything.

I couldn't see if Quinn had his own weapon with him, and the stranger didn't have anything I recognized as useful.

Besides, with my luck, I'd probably bring the cave ceiling down around us.

Snarling, now growling, they kept attacking each other, neither willing to back down.

Both bled freely, Quinn's suit and the stranger's shirt both in bloody tatters.

Oh god.

They were going to kill each other.

If I didn't find a way to stop this, Quinn was going to die.

The thought alone was enough to seize my chest with icy fingers that had nothing to do with the weather.

In desperation, I grabbed one of the rocks from around the fire and flung it towards them, but Quinn batted it away without really noticing.

I threw another, then another, none of the missiles doing enough damage to break their deadly concentration.

Then, careless in my haste, I reached too close to the fire.

In an instant, the cuff of my suit caught, smoldering.

"Quinn!" I shrieked in terror as the flames began to flare. "Help!"

Suddenly, they were both at my side, Quinn pulling the suit off my torso, while the stranger wrapped my arm in one of the still-wet hides.

"Is she hurt?" he growled.

"She better not be," Quinn snarled. "She better not need a healing wand."

They glared at each other.

"Hell of a way to say hello," Quinn said when he was finally certain that I was unscathed. He rocked back to sit cross-legged in front of the fire, tugging me gently to sit beside him.

"This first." Carefully, the stranger pulled up the damp gorin pelt and I winced, unwilling to look. But the skin was only slightly reddened.

"You're gonna need the healing wand more than I will," I muttered, looking at the wreck of Quinn's chest. "Planning to make this a habit?"

The stranger snorted. "He'll be fine. We always are."

"Who the hell is 'we'?" I snapped, tired of the mystery and the secrets. "And who the hell are you?"

The mystery man smiled crookedly. "Sorry, I figured if you were his mate, you knew. I guess we never did get around to introductions. I'm Torik."

Wait, mate?

He continued. "I'm assuming you know my idiot brother."

What? I turned to Quinn, stunned. "He's your brother? Why were you trying to kill him?"

He shrugged. "He took you. I wasn't really thinking clearly after that."

I struggled to stand up, to try to get some space between me and the two obviously insane men, but Quinn just pulled me into his lap.

"It's been a long hour hunting you down." He nuzzled the side of my neck. "When I saw you were gone...Let me just hold you for a little bit."

"Sure, we can do that," I said, the catch in his voice revealing how worried he'd been.

Honestly, now that he was here, all my fears faded away.

Maybe it was the exhaustion of the rollercoaster of emotions and the throbbing pain in my arm.

Maybe we'd kept each other up a little late last night.

But now he was here, with me.

And whatever happened, we were more than able to handle it.

Together.

QUINN

With Trini safe and dozing in my arms, the rage that had burned inside me settled to a simmer.

"What are you doing here?" I asked Torik. "I understand keeping a low profile, but this seems like taking things to the extreme."

"Hold that thought." Torik wandered further back into the cave where I could see the long sleek shape of the planet hopper.

Liquid sounds and metal clinks came shortly thereafter. He came back and handed me a short glass, careful not to disturb Trini.

He took a sip and made a face. "Not as good as her korvasian brandy," he nodded towards Trini, "but it'll do."

Just raising the glass to my face made my eyes water. "How long have you been here?" I gasped. "Doc's going to have to rebuild your gut."

"I'm guessing my messages didn't make it past sector security?" he asked as he settled back down across the fire from us. "It's been…a while."

"Nope, just recently got bits and pieces of it. Enough to get us to this planet but no further."

He sighed, took a long drink. "We took a contract with NewTronic Industries. Three, maybe four years ago. It's been a little hard to keep track of time here. Sorry, it makes for a crappy report. Anyhow, ten of us went on the job." His eyes narrowed at something I couldn't see. "Long story short, it all went to hell, and we had to split up."

"Do you know where the others are?" I took a drink, trying not to stand up and shout at the news.

Ten more of us that might have survived.

Might.

"We agreed to run silent," he answered. "No communication to betray us to any of the corps. I managed to get this far, but my hopper's engines got knocked off-line. I fixed it up enough to get back and forth to the city, but not enough to make the jump all the way back to the *Daedalus*." He shook his head. "Doc must be out of her mind, but I'll be glad enough to see her that I'll let her fuss all she'd like."

"I don't think she's going to scold you much," I said quietly.

Somehow, I hadn't thought this part of the mission all the way through. I took a deep breath and dove in. "She's lost too many of us."

As quickly as I could, I told him about the Hunters, how we'd been trapped on the *Star* and slaughtered, and General Melchior's mad plan to take over the Empire and its tragic conclusion.

Torik took another long drink and pushed his shaggy hair out of his eyes. "So you're telling me we're working for the Empire now? Doc must hate that."

"That's what you got out of all that?" I asked, feeling hollow-chested at having to walk through the horror those years had been.

"Nope, but it's about all I can take in right now." He glanced down at Trini. "How much does she know?"

"Not enough, not yet," I confessed.

"The way you're acting around her, I figure you better get on that." His lips twisted into a half smile.

"Yeah," I stroked her hair and she nestled into my shoulder. "I'll have to tell her, but the way things are between the Areitis Sector and the Empire, not sure how she's gonna feel about leaving."

"If she's your mate, what choice do you have?"

I sat, considering his words.

Last night I'd half admitted it to myself, wondered at the possibility.

My mate.

It seemed impossible, too much wishing to be real.

But today, when I'd realized she was gone, the wrench that ran through me tore me apart.

There was no question.

Trini was my mate.

And whether she would have me or not, it was going to make things more complicated.

"Plenty of time to tell her on the way back into town," I told Torik. "Mack's in upper orbit, waiting to pick us up when we give the word, but she's got a friend that I know she's going to want to check on pretty soon."

"Mack?" He looked confused.

"Sorry, Killian. That's a whole 'nother story."

Torik nodded. "I can see I've missed a lot of stories." He tapped his fingers on his glass. "If it's not a bother, I won't be ready to leave for a few days. I can meet you in town, at her place."

"Seriously? I thought you wanted out of here?" I took another drink and winced. "Or is it too much fun playing with the gorin?"

"Somebody's gotta do it, or they're going to start heading south," he shrugged. "And yes, I'm more than ready to head out, but figured while I was stuck here, I might as well play a little game of my own. Can you give me a few more days to wrap it up?"

I thought about the conversation I was going to have with Trini, how she'd want to be sure Russar was fine, see Risti.

Who knew how many other friends she had scattered around the city?

Her life was here. Her work, her friends.

And I was going to try to convince her to leave it all behind.

I'd need every day I could get.

"We've got a few things to wrap up, as well," was all I answered. "Let's say two days? But not at the Merry Stormcloud. Do you know the cone shop up the street with the pink door?"

Torik shook his head, amused. "If she got you to eat one of those things, she really is your mate." He held a hand out for my glass. "Come on, let me give you a ride back to your cruiser." He cocked his head to the side. "You did stop to seal it up before you started chasing me, didn't you?"

I stopped, mind blank. "Honestly, I'm not sure. Once I saw that she was gone, well..."

Torik laughed. "If you've got any unexpected visitors, I'll give you a hand."

I bent over Trini's head. I hated to wake her:

kidnapped, dragged off through a blizzard, and nearly burned, it'd been a hell of a day for her.

"Come on, honey, it's time to go."

"Don't wanna. Comfy," she mumbled.

That was fine by me. The longer I held her close, the steadier my thoughts were, the more relaxed I felt.

"Good thing I like carrying you," I whispered.

Carefully I stood, but as I readjusted her in my arms, her eyelids fluttered open. "Wait? Where are we going? Neither of us are exactly dressed for the cold."

It was true. We were going through insulated suits at a remarkable rate.

"Won't need them," I explained. "He's giving us a ride back to the cruiser."

She shook her head, frowning. "You can let me down now, I'm awake."

With reluctance, I set her on her feet.

"If this is how it always is when just brothers meet, I'd hate to see a full family reunion," she teased.

"Sorry about that," Torik said. "But yeah, we can actually get a little rowdy, I guess. Especially since it's all guys."

"Less rowdy these days," I corrected him. "More than a few ladies around. The baby is probably the noisiest of us all, really."

"Baby!" Torik paled. "You didn't mention that part."

I grinned, glad to be thinking about all of the good

changes that had happened, not just the struggles.

"Think of all the things you have to look forward to when you get home."

Looking at it, I realized it had been a miracle Torik had fixed up the hopper enough to be able to make the run to the city and back.

"No wonder you couldn't get off-planet once you were down," I said, looking at the long scorch mark down the side of the engine casing.

"Yeah," Torik said. "Would've been handy to have Hakon around. Not my best day." He slid into the cockpit and started flipping switches.

Trini strapped herself into a seat in the back. "I still don't understand why you decided to live up here. Surely you could have found something to do in Rondi, or even one of the smaller settlements?"

"I get a little antsy around too many people," Torik admitted. "Besides, somebody's gotta keep the monster packs in check or they're going to start eating settlers."

Trini shuddered. "Good point. But, if you're coming back with Quinn, who's going to do that?"

"I'll try to set something up, I promise," Torik said.

And then the meaning of Trini's words hit.

I hadn't told her yet that Torik was coming back with me.

How much had she overheard when I thought she was sleeping?

TRINI

The trip back to the cruiser in Torik's hopper was cramped. But it didn't matter.

I had far too much on my mind to worry about it.

When Torik and Quinn had been talking, I'd been dozing in and out.

The fire was warm and knowing I was safe with Quinn made it easy to give into the exhaustion, fall into a half-sleep.

But the story Quinn had told Torik was something out of a nightmare.

I'd known the world of the Empire was strange, but that was beyond anything I'd ever heard of.

It was impossible to believe.

And yet...

Everything made so much more sense now

Illegal levels of genetic modification.

That was the only answer to be read between the lines, once you took out all the battles and the machinations.

Quinn and Torik both. Possibly their entire family.

Not quite human.

That must have been what Dr. Jaylan saw when he looked at Quinn through those lenses, some invisible clue that whoever had ... was it built? created? ... changed Quinn and Torik was a brilliant genetic scientist.

But when it came down to it, did it matter?

I studied the back of Quinn's head, where he and Torik leaned over the cockpit controls.

Quinn had taken care of Russar when he was stabbed. Comforted me when I was afraid.

Won a stupid stuffed toy for me, just because I wanted it.

Was being human something decided by your DNA or your actions?

Who was I to say who qualified and who didn't?

"Looks like you had some company down there," Torik commented as the hopper took a low circle over the cruiser.

The blizzard had cleared and I could see countless tracks from where the gorin had circled our ship, long scratches down the side.

"Huh," Quinn said. "Looks like I locked up after all, even when distracted."

And that was something else that was going to take some thinking about.

Mate.

Technically, I supposed what we did last night in the cruiser qualified as mating, but the way Quinn and Torik used the word, it obviously meant something else.

Something important.

Quinn turned his head back. "You alright to stay here with this jerk while I go check things out?" he asked.

"Of course. I don't think he's going to try to kidnap me again."

The worry in his eyes made me regret the tease. "I'll be fine. Go do whatever you need to do," I shooed him on.

Grin flashing, he jumped out, closing the door to the hopper quickly behind him to keep the slight warmth inside.

Silence sat heavy in the hopper.

"He's a good man," Torik said, staring ahead through the viewscreen. "Try not to be too hard on him, okay?"

"Don't I get any choice in this?" I asked softly.

Torik spun as far as he could in the seat. "Of course you do!" he said looking confused. "Whatever you decide is your decision, no one else's. I'm just, well," he reddened, turned back to face the front. "Just trying to give you information."

"What if I don't go back with him," I asked, my heart already breaking a little at the thought of leaving home, the family I'd built here in the city, my aunt and uncles in the south. "What if I can't?"

"He won't force you to do anything," Torik answered just as quietly. "No matter what it does to him. But nothing says leaving would be forever." He leaned back in the seat, and I caught a glimpse of his face. Not angry, bitter. "I got stuck here for too long because the rest of the Pack was busy dealing with another problem and never even got my messages. I suspect if you wanted anything, the moon on a platter or a space station for jewelry, he'd get it for you. If you wanted to travel back and forth between the Empire and the sector, he'd find a way."

I blinked, mind spinning.

That was even more to take in.

And somehow, even more frightening.

Quinn rapped on the window. "All clear," he said. As he leaned in to pick me up, I pulled away.

"What's wrong?" he asked, expression blank.

I blushed, ashamed of myself for my own reaction. "I'm capable of walking, you know." I insisted.

"Right," he said slowly. "I know that. But I figured

you're not really dressed for the cold, and I can get you inside the cruiser faster if I carry you." He gave a slight smile. "Heat's already on and everything."

"I'll say goodbye here," Torik said. "See you in town."

Quinn was right.

The storm may have moved on, but it was bitterly cold as we dashed the short distance across the trampled snow and up the ramp into the cruiser.

As the door sealed behind us, I could hear the rumble of the hopper's engines as Torik took off, heading back to his lair.

"I'm..." This was ridiculous, but for the first time, conversation didn't flow easily between us. "I'm going to go get changed," I finished lamely.

Quinn said nothing as I bolted back through the lounge to the first bedroom we'd slept in.

Digging through the bag I'd packed back at the Merry Stormcloud, which seemed like a lifetime ago, I pulled out fresh clothes. A warm comfy sweater and soft, well-broken-in pants.

I used the replicator to generate a set of thick, fuzzy blue socks. Apparently in my haste, I'd forgotten a few things. What can I say? It was a busy night.

When I came back out to the lounge, Quinn stood awkwardly by the table. "I didn't know if you wanted food, or if you needed to get some more sleep."

"Food would be good," I agreed.

We ate quietly, no laughing, no joking.

Careful not to touch, not meeting each other's eyes.

Every bite felt like it stuck in my throat.

When we finished, Quinn put the dishes in the recycler. "I'll program the route in. You should get some more rest." And without a look back, he headed to the cockpit.

I sat at the table.

This was up to me.

What did I want?

I punched up a steaming mug of chocolate, then paused. Altered the reference recipe for a second serving.

More chocolate was never a bad thing.

The hot mugs in my hand, I headed down the stairs to the cockpit and handed the second one to Quinn.

"What's this?"

I settled into the seat beside him and took a long sip of the rich, creamy goodness. "Trust me, you'll like it better than cones. I promise."

He gave me another one of those quick smiles and took a sip. He blinked. "It's, it's actually good!"

We sat in silence as the cruiser rolled south for long minutes, just drinking our chocolate. Mine, sweetened.

His not.

Different.

Still chocolate.

"When were you going to tell me?" I asked quietly, still staring at the white world outside.

"Until last night, I didn't realize I needed to," he answered. "It's not something we talk about much." He took another sip, glanced my way. "I never meant to lie to you."

"You didn't," I admitted. "It never exactly came up. It's just ...kind of a surprise, you know?"

Miles rolled by, and the silence became less tense, more companionable.

"It doesn't bother you?" he finally asked.

I'd circled around it for hours, brain chewing on the issue.

And now that it was time to say something, the answer was clear.

"No. You're still you. I don't understand what was done to you, but it doesn't change anything."

He winced. "Does it change if nothing was done to me, if I've always been like this?"

I sat with it for a moment.

Weighed the idea.

"Nope. You're still you, born or made." I looked over at him, long and steadily. "And I like you. So luckily, that works out."

His shoulders sank, and I realized how easy it would have been to hurt him, to hurt this fragile thing between us, with a careless word.

"So...since you like me," he took a sip as his cheeks colored, "do you think it could be more than that some day?"

I took a sip of my own chocolate and gave myself time to think.

This is what adults did, wasn't it? Talked things over rationally?

But it didn't feel adult. It felt awful.

"I think so," I said slowly.

His face lit up and I continued hurriedly.

"But you've got to understand, we've only known each other a few days. And while I feel something that draws me to you, I need time." I took a deep breath. "And I don't know if I can leave Heladae."

I was sick to my gut, as if I had stabbed him like those goons had Russar, and twisted the knife.

"That's reasonable," he forced himself to say. "Give me time to change your mind?"

"I haven't made it up yet," I reassured him. "I just don't know what to do."

"Then we need a plan of action. First thing," he said decisively, "we should get the healing wand on your arm and probably over your ankle again. Should have done that when we got in."

"You never did use it on yourself, did you?" I teased.

He ran his fingers through his hair, looking bashful.

"That, that I did actually lie about. Sorry."

I laughed as I gathered our mugs and led the way back to the galley. "Probably for the best. Having all of this in my brain, then meeting the monsters? Might have been a little much to take in."

"By monsters, do you mean the monsters or my brother?

I laughed. "I can't imagine what your family is like, I know…"

I paused, thinking of the story he had told Torik.

Of how many they'd lost.

"I know it's been hard lately, but the idea of so many of you together, you sound like you're happy now."

"It's not just the brothers," he said quietly, wrapping his arms around me. "We weren't a family before. Not really. But when the mates came, they shaped things up."

He grabbed the healing wand from the drawer and led me back to the second bedroom, the one where we'd slept.

Where I'd been content. Happy.

This time I managed to pull off my own boots. "Are all of your brothers mated?" I wondered.

"No," he froze. "At least, I don't think so. It's hard to tell."

"If I'm going to understand anything about this mate business," I said, poking his shoulder, "you have to understand it first."

"No, I know who's mated. It's just... We thought the ten of us were the only survivors. But if a whole squad is still somewhere in the Areitis Sector?"

As he ran the healing wand over my arm, the reddened skin faded away until not even the faintest twinge remained.

Suddenly I yawned, the events of the day catching up with me again.

"Come to bed," I said, patting the covers as I pulled off my socks and crawled under the covers. "Tell me happy stories about your family. Your new family with all the people you've picked up along the way."

He chuckled, then slipped off his boots and pants and slipped into the bed, wrapping me in his arms.

Mate.

I might not know what it meant, but I knew that right here, right now, I felt like I was home.

"Let me tell you about the time that Granny Z decided she was going to teach little Vicki the basics of interstellar piracy..."

QUINN

As we got closer to the city, I glanced at Trini.

She'd been quiet today, but that could just have been from being on the run.

She wasn't used to this life.

And I didn't want her to be.

"We should ditch the cruiser outside of town," I announced. "I'm good, but we got lucky getting out of that complex. I'm not looking forward to reversing the trick."

Trini pulled up a map on the tablet, tapped a space to the northeast of town. "There's not a lot of folks out this way. It'd be a bit of a walk to get back, but it shouldn't take too long."

She looked at me and rolled her eyes. "Don't tell me. Is that where you set down when you first came in?"

"A little further out this way," I replied, tapping a bit to the west. "Pretty close. I didn't mind the walk."

Dry rolling hills covered the land to the west of town.

I would rather have found a canyon, a cave, something with a bit more cover to leave the cruiser, but I had to trust that it's adaptive camouflage would keep it hidden.

"Don't plan on needing it anytime soon, but I'd rather not leave anything that could point to us."

As we hiked back in, Trini kept fidgeting with the strap of her bag.

"I can carry that," I offered. Maybe for the sixth time, or the seventh.

"I know you can, I'm just worried. I know we can't just comm Dr. Jaylan, but what if Russar didn't make it? What am I ever going to tell Paulo?"

I wrapped her hand in mine.

"And that's why we're going there first thing. We don't know if anyone is still looking for you. And the Fourth Quarter is as good a place as any to hide out, I'd bet."

WE HAD to circle through town a bit until I recognized one of the streets the gang had led us through on the way to Dr. Jaylan's.

After that, it was easy.

I banged on the door while Trini shifted nervously on her feet.

"He'll be fine," I said, hoping that my words wouldn't prove to be a lie.

"If he's fixing up the guys around here on a regular basis, Jaylan's had plenty of practice on gut wounds." I added.

Maybe that wasn't as encouraging as I had hoped.

But it didn't matter, because suddenly the door was flung open.

"Thank the gods of surgery and precision," Jaylan grumbled. "If you hadn't come back for another day, I would've been tempted to sedate him just for my sanity's sake."

He turned to go back into the building, and we followed. "I had forgotten what a terrible patient he always was."

"Who is it?" bellowed Russar. "I need to get back to my place. Get me unstrapped from this thing!"

Trini went running towards the shouting. "You stay right where you are," she scolded. "You didn't see how bad you were hurt."

The doctor and I followed at a more sedate pace.

"She was a little worried," I commented.

"Well, she had a reason to be," Jaylan admitted. "He lost a lot of blood. It's one thing to patch up a younger man, a little harder as the body ages." He shot a glance at me. "Or is it?"

I shrugged, uncomfortable. "Not a doctor. Wouldn't know." I took a breath and reminded myself we owed a favor. "But I know somebody you can ask. Thank you."

By the time we reached Trini and Russar, she was already arguing with him.

"She's not going back to the bar, not anytime soon," I cut in. "She's who they were looking for to start with. You were just collateral damage."

"How could you say such a thing!" Trini protested.

But Russar laughed. "The boy is probably right. Though I've been betting they were actually after him."

Trini shook her head. "No question about that. They were trying pretty hard to get me. We were both lucky Quinn was there."

Grudgingly, Russar held his hand out. "Then I owe you. For taking care of her, and apparently me." He scowled at Jaylan. "And if this bastard would let me get back on my feet, I could go take care of the bar myself."

Jaylan passed the reclining med-bench Russar was strapped to and went to check the consoles.

"Spent too much time fixing you up. I've got a deal

with that one," he nodded in my direction, "to keep you fixed up. Don't go ruining my work."

"Now what are we going to do?" Russar grumbled.

Trini tapped her fingers to her neck, thinking. "Don't Ondar and Feevo owe quite a bit on their tabs?" she asked Russar. "Why don't you comm them, let them know they can work it off in exchange for going in and setting the place to rights."

"Humph," Russar said. "Probably drink all the stock."

"I don't think so," Trini said brightly. "I think they know you'd find them. And they'd be very, very sorry."

"Maybe." Russar didn't look convinced, but at least he wasn't still trying to figure out how to unfasten himself from the med-bench.

"But that brings up another problem." I turned to Jaylan. "Know a place we could stay around here?"

"Does it look like I'm running a hotel?" he snapped. "My patients have immunity. But you? You'd have to pay a tithe."

"And by pay," I said slowly, "you mean trade a favor."

"Didn't think you were dumb," Jaylan said. "I'm sure Venac will be here soon. You couldn't have crossed into his territory without him finding out."

"Great," I said. "That'll keep me from having to go look for him."

And either the doctor had signaled the gang leader or he just had a good sense of timing, because no more than a minute passed when there was a banging at the front door.

"Back and forth, all day," Jaylan muttered as he went to the door.

I wasn't surprised that the man he led back was the gang leader who had brought us to the doctor three nights before.

"Word is out Mada Sommu is looking for you," the newcomer said.

But he wasn't looking at me, he was watching Trini.

"Word should be, nobody's going to find her," I corrected him.

He grinned. "You're big, I'll give you that. Look like you could handle yourself in a fight. But do you really think you can keep us from taking her? The reward is pretty good looking, too."

Trini stepped to my side quickly and put her hand on my arm. "I *know* he could stop you. And unless you really want what I suspect is the only medical care you have around here to be destroyed, you'll stop, and talk reasonably."

Venac jerked his head back as if he'd been hit, then twisted his lips into a sneer. "Well, everything is possible for friends. And you know..."

Trini sighed. "Yes, I'm sure. Friends do each other favors. What do you want? You know we need a safe place to stay, in silence. What do you want in return?"

Venac looked at me, eyebrows raised. "Do you always let the lady do the talking?"

"Don't see why not," I responded, and wrapped an arm around her shoulders, thankful for her presence. Just having her near was enough to cool the rage that had threatened to take over. "Besides, I'm curious, too. What *do* you want?"

"Well, I'd have to think about it." The man made a show of thinking, but I was sure he had every word planned out, had from the moment he knew we were back in his territory.

You didn't get to the top of a gang like that and be stupid.

At least, you didn't stay at the top.

"Really, we're talking about two favors, aren't we?" He held up one finger. "First, for not turning her in and telling everybody she's off-limits. Really, the reward is tempting. It's gonna take some convincing."

I didn't bother trying to smother the growl this time. "I would be happy to help with the convincing."

Venac continued, holding up another finger. "And then, you need a place to stay, if I understand right. Someplace kinda quiet, right?" He brought his hand back down and shrugged. "Like I said, two favors."

"You're still not telling me anything I can work with. What. Do. You. Want?"

"You don't really do friendly very well, do you?" he said, shaking his head in mock sorrow.

"No."

"Doesn't really matter to me. See, we've got a little bit of a situation that's come up in the quarter." He leaned against one of the consoles, and Jaylan promptly shooed him away. "Use a chair, you idiot. That's sensitive equipment."

Venac at least had the sense to look a little bit abashed "Sorry about that, Doc. As I was saying, we've had some newcomers. They've been making some noise."

"A shakedown job?" It wouldn't be the first time. When the Pack had been running as straight-out mercenaries on the *Daedalus*, we'd taken all kinds of jobs.

We weren't always the good guys.

Thinking about it, I'm pretty sure we usually weren't.

"Nah, my fellows can take care of that." His eyes narrowed. "But the thing is, they took something, someone. I want her back. Everyone knows who my guys are. But you're new enough you might be able to slip through their defenses."

"When you say her..." Trini started, I could tell she was trying to find appropriately delicate phrasing. "Are you one hundred percent certain that she didn't just leave you?"

Venac scowled at her, confused. "What are you talking about? My Nonna wouldn't leave me. She's the heart and soul of the quarter." His face twisted angrily. "No, those bastards know that by keeping her hidden, they have a handle on me. Can't have that. Besides, how do I know they're treating her right? They don't even know what her favorite foods are."

"Wait," I interrupted the unexpected deluge of information. "Are we talking about your daughter?"

Trini slipped from my side to walk up to Venac and before I could stop her, she put her hand on his shoulder. "I'm so sorry about your grandmother. We'll help get her back."

"Grandmother, sure," I said, catching up. "We, not so much," I hurried on, avoiding Trini's glare. "Whatever's going on here, wherever we're going," I corrected myself quickly "— I'm going alone. You're staying wherever we find a safe place."

Trini put her hand on her hip and rolled her eyes at me. "Exactly how much experience do you have with crotchety old women?"

"You'd be surprised," I groaned.

And in that moment, I realized she was gonna fit in with the rest of the mates just fine.

TRINI

"**N**ot what you're used to, is it?" Venac sneered.

I was starting to think it was just his normal tone of voice.

When we'd brought Russar, bleeding and dying in Quinn's arms, to Doctor Jaylan's building, everything had been too dark to see. I'd been too scared after the attempted abduction to even look around.

Coming in earlier today, I'd been too distracted and worried to notice anything other than how long it seemed to be taking.

So now I was observing the Fourth Quarter really for the first time.

It was run down, sure. But the hives looked well-equipped, the people on the streets didn't look miserable or hungry.

"The only difference I can tell between here and the rest of the city is you've got fewer tourists," I answered mildly. "I don't see how that's a bad thing, to be honest."

"Ha," Venac snorted, clearly not convinced.

Quinn trailed us, a half-step away from looming.

"Tell me more about your grandmother?" I asked, hoping to forestall a further confrontation between the two men. "How do you know she was taken? And who took her?"

Then he pulled a scrap of fabric from his pocket and ran it lovingly through his fingers.

Red, blue, and purple paisley patterns. Even the scrap, no bigger than my hand, was bright enough I had to blink.

"It's from her favorite headscarf," Venac said gruffly. "Trust me. She's the only one that has one like it."

"I believe you," I murmured.

"They sent it with a note?" Quinn asked.

Venac shot a look over his shoulder and nodded. "Got it in one. They sent it this morning. Didn't ask for anything, didn't threaten. Just said she'd be their guest for a while."

We turned down another street. A woman and two children crossed the street in front of us. She nodded quickly to Venac, and it was interesting to notice that she didn't look scared, just respectful.

Something to think about later.

"What do you think they want?" Quinn asked.

"No idea, but I'm not gonna like it."

"But how did they even get her? I'm learning what it's like to have someone want to watch over your every move."

Quinn reached forward and tousled my hair, and I resisted the urge to stick my tongue out at him. "I'm pretty sure you would act the same way with your grandmother, wouldn't you?"

A muscle jumped in Venac's jaw.

"Of course. But Nonna does what she wants. Always has."

We turned again down a slightly narrower street and the buildings here had fewer windows, with grills over the ones I could see.

"She doesn't like those replicators, never has. Keeps a small garden plot behind the little house she and my grandfather lived in when they were first married."

A man stepped out from the doorway and nodded sharply to Venac. He seemed to wait a second for orders, then stepped back, fading away when he received none.

Or at least, none that I saw.

"One of my boys goes with her, we didn't think about it too much. These days, it's more to take over any digging or raking she wants done." He shrugged lightly, his voice still tight. "It's an honored position. A reward, a show of trust."

"And somebody betrayed that, didn't they?" Quinn commented.

"Where you're from," Venac raised a hand, "and don't tell me, I don't care that much. I don't think you deal much with the bright shiny parts of the Void or of people, either."

"Not usually, no," was all that Quinn answered.

"And that's why I can't send any of my regular guys to get her back. Hosk, the bastard, would recognize anyone I work with, anyone I do business with."

"Are you sure he's still with the newcomers?" I asked.

We stopped, and Venac rapped a pattern on the metal door of the building to the left.

Waited, and knocked out a second pattern.

A woman's voice came from a small speaker set high into the wall. "It's what the cameras are for, dummy. Somebody might know the code, but they'd be an idiot to use your face."

Without further abuse, the door slid open.

"Doesn't hurt to do it both ways," Venac hollered into the recesses of the house.

Unlike Jaylan's cavernous warehouse, this seemed to be a perfectly ordinary home.

If not having any windows was normal.

And I suspected a large number of weapons were hidden within easy reach of those who might need them.

"Bring them on back," the woman called out again. "Nobody trailed you."

"And that's how we're sure Hosk is still with the strangers," Venac declared, gesturing for me to precede him.

"They've got their cameras set up, so do we. We haven't seen him since he disappeared with Nonna."

We passed through a narrow beige hallway until the room opened into a brightly lit dining room.

Or, I guess it had been a dining room once.

The large wooden table was covered with scattered tablets, and screens lined the walls. Each screen was quartered, rotating through different views of the neighborhood.

And ruling over it all was a tall woman, her iron gray hair cropped short. She wore tan pants and a black sleeveless tank top.

"Thanks for agreeing to help us out," she said.

"Your brother didn't give us much choice," Quinn answered.

I looked between the two of them, then spun back to look at him. "They don't look anything alike."

The woman glared at Venac. "How much talking did you do on the way over?"

"Either that or close cousins," Quinn continued. "As family oriented as our host is, it made sense. The shapes of their skulls, particularly around the eye sockets, have certain similar characteristics."

I rocked back on my heels slightly. "Honey, I don't think it's polite to talk about people's skull shapes."

"I'll try to remember that," Quinn said.

I think he was joking.

Maybe.

"Whatever, it's not a secret," she held her hand out and for the first , I noticed that her right arm from slightly below the shoulder down was softly shaded metal. "Sola."

Quinn shook it without hesitation. "What sort of clamp strength do you get with that?"

"Enough to rip your arm off," she said, baring her teeth in something approximating a smile.

"Great." He turned to the screens. "So, I assume that from here you've got surveillance on what our target is?"

"Everything you could want and then some." She opened more screens, more views, until I was dizzy. "I just can't figure out how we get in."

"That, that I would want, actually," Quinn said. "Let's see what you've got. Where are they in town?"

He pulled a chair out for me and stood behind me with his hands on my shoulders, warm and strong.

But his voice was cold, all business.

"They took over the Pythons' old place," Venac started, pulling up another chair. "It was smart. We'd wiped them out years ago but the building was still there, wouldn't have taken too much to make it defensible again."

"We've sent over drones with heat sensors, but they keep getting picked off," Sola said, grabbing one of the tablets. "What windows they have are all blastproof plexi. Still, I've been able to pick up enough movement to map out the interior with some detail." With a pulling motion of her fingers, she raised her hand above the tablet and a 3D model of the building appeared in the air before her.

She sent it spinning slowly before us. "This looks like the areas they guard most. And I'd bet this internal room must be where they're keeping her."

"This doesn't sound like just another gang takeover," Quinn said. "What do you really think is going on?"

Sola and Venac glanced at each other, apparently silently continuing a long-standing argument.

Finally, Sola spoke. "I think they're Mada's people. She's always hated not having total control of Rondi."

My stomach clenched and Quinn's hands briefly tightened on my shoulders.

Not who I wanted us to be tangling with.

But if she'd taken some harmless little old woman, that just wasn't right.

That had nothing to do with running her business interests, nothing to do with keeping her investments secure.

Nothing to do with whatever she thought Makkar had stolen from her.

This just wasn't right.

"We've driven off invaders before, we've kept our control of the Fourth Quarter for three generations now," Venac added. "Made it a good place, maybe a little rough, but a place people can make a living that's not dependent on the corporations."

Sola ran her hands through her short hair. "We've got enough favors spread out around town that even if it was someone else from the city trying to make a move, we would've heard it. No way we wouldn't have."

Quinn took the chair next to me and grabbed the model, drew his hands apart to enlarge it, and studied it closely. "What kind of armaments do they have?"

"That's the other thing that makes me think it's Mada," Sola replied, nodding slowly. "They've got good ones. Enforcer quality. And no other corp would dare set up an outpost here. It might as well be declaring war on her."

Quinn grabbed another tablet and ran through endless specs that made no sense to me.

Finally, he sat back in the chair, silent for long moments, his expression distant.

"I'll do it, but no more talk of this favors business." His eyes narrowed and he glared at Venac. "I'll get your grandmother back, if she's there. But you'll keep Trini safe. Here. No more talk of turning her in to Mada for the reward."

"What?" Sola threw a tablet at her brother. Luckily, she used her natural arm, so it didn't hit him too hard. "You did not!" she exclaimed.

"It seemed like it was worth trying," Venac said, rubbing his shoulder. "Never want to give up leverage, right?"

"Of course we'll keep her safe," Sola answered Quinn, ignoring her brother. "I wish we could send more people with you, but all of our fighters are known to Hosk. If they were spotted, it'd be a dead giveaway that an attack was coming."

"I should go with you," I said quietly.

"Not happening," Quinn growled.

"How are you planning to get her back here safely while making sure no one is following you?" I pressed on. "What if she's injured, or confused? You're going to need help."

"We can have our people hidden, ready to cover him on the way out," Sola said.

"Hidden where?" I argued. "Are you sure Hosk doesn't know about whatever locations you'd use?"

Sola looked at me appraisingly. "You don't look like much of a fighter."

I laughed. "I'm not. But I don't like people getting pushed around. And if Quinn has to split his attention between guiding your grandmother back here and fighting off attackers, that just increases his chances of getting killed."

My throat tightened and my breath caught.

"And I can't have that."

QUINN

"I'll leave a couple of hours before dawn." I said, pushing away from the table, my head full of maps and scans.

Sola nodded. "Whatever my idiot brother says, we appreciate it." She rose. "You'll need to eat first, come on. We haven't used this room for meals in years, too big."

Trini stayed quiet through dinner.

There was no point in trying to change her mind.

I'd try persuading her later.

Honestly, none of us were feeling particularly talkative.

There wasn't enough information to make anything other than the most minimal plan, and none of us were in the mood for idle chatter.

As Venac took the dishes to put into the recycler, Trini held hers for just a moment.

"What about Russar? Is he in any danger?"

Venac smiled, the first relaxed, real smile I think he'd given us yet. "He was a legend in the fighting pits. The only danger he's in here is from somebody trying to get too close asking for an autograph when he's feeling crappy."

A ghost of the smile flitted across Trini's features. "Good to hear."

I stood, holding out my hand for hers. "We should get some rest before heading out."

"I'll show you to your room," Sola said. "But one thing first."

A tall wooden chest stood at the end of the hallway. She opened a drawer, rummaged around for a moment until she found something, and held it out. "Take this with you."

About the length of my hand, it was a glossy black rectangle, inlaid with silver swirls.

"It's lovely, but what is it?" Trini asked.

"A little small to be much of a weapon," I commented, turning it over to examine it more closely.

Sola smiled, but that didn't soften the fine lines of strain around her eyes. "It's a token. Mada's goons don't know you, Hosk doesn't know you, but neither does my grandmother. This way she'll know we sent you."

I took it and slipped it into my pocket. "Good idea."

The house didn't have an elevator. Instead, a spiral staircase led us up one level, then another.

"Mostly empty or storage now," Sola said as she pushed open a door. "My grandfather loved keeping everybody in one house, but it's just Venac and me now. Makes it easier if we need to stash someone for a little bit, though."

She gave the room a glance, as if to ensure everything was where she expected it to be. I couldn't imagine the furniture risking her displeasure enough to get dusty.

After Sola closed the door behind us, Trini placed her bag on the dresser, her expression remote.

I came up behind her and wrapped my arms around her waist, bending over to nuzzle the crook of her neck where it met her shoulder, breathing in the sweet scent of her.

"You're not going to talk me out of it," she said, even as she leaned back into my embrace.

"I can try," I answered, pulling her tighter against me.

The wall of ice she'd encased herself in finally cracked as she wiggled to turn into my arms, winding her arms around my neck.

"I could try to talk you out of it, too," she said, tilting her face up and parting her lips.

"You could," I admitted. "But neither of us would really win that game, would we?"

"I've got a better game in mind," she teased, and I fell upon her lips, kissing and licking down the side of her throat, tugging the shirt off her shoulder.

She pushed me away. "My game, my rules." Her eyes were lit with mischief as she pulled off her top, then started on mine. "Think you can let me do that?"

"I'll let you do anything you want," I breathed. And I would.

Once we were finally undressed, she pushed me back until my knees hit the edge of the bed. Another tiny push and I sat, pulling her into my lap as I fell.

"Was this what you had in mind?" I growled, unable to keep from grinding against her sweet heat.

"Something like that," she answered, then rose on her knees, straddling my lap.

And with mind-blasting slowness, lowered her slick folds on my cock.

No battle had ever been so difficult as the one I fought to stay still, to not give in to the urge to thrust against her.

Finally, she was fully seated, trembling and panting. "Trini," I groaned. "I can't do this forever."

"Can you do this?" she asked, rocking her hips against me, and the world exploded into pleasure as I knotted my fingers against her hips and drove into her.

Gentle deliberation grew into frenzy as we spiraled together, then over the edge, my every nerve shattered by her very touch.

We collapsed back on the bed, and still, I couldn't let her go.

Wouldn't.

"Can you promise me that you can get in and out of that fortress without anyone noticing? Even while you're dealing with a frightened, potentially injured, elderly woman?" she whispered in the dark.

I sighed, but I'd promised not to lie. Not even by omission. Not anymore.

"No."

"Then you need someone else," she insisted. "Maybe not inside, but someone to bring their Nonna back here to free you up for fighting."

"I don't like it," I said. "I hate it, actually."

"But I'm right, aren't I?" she insisted. "And I hate it, too."

"Does it help if I tell you it doesn't look like it's much of a fortress?"

She laughed and reached down for the covers, pulling them over us. "Not really. It just makes me wonder what your life is like that you actually have definitions." Stifling a yawn, she snuggled into my side. "What qualifies something as a fortress rather than just a hideout, anyway?"

WE LEFT in the early hours before dawn.

Venac and Sola met us in the war room. "We'll watch as far as we can on the cameras," she said. "I've got comms out to all of our people to be aware of the situation. They'll keep the streets clear for you if they can."

"Appreciated," I said.

For a change, Trini wasn't interested in her kaf. "It'll just hurt my stomach now," she said. "Come on, sooner we're done, sooner home, and then we can enjoy it."

I took her hand in mine, kissed the inside of her wrist, just to have the taste of her. "Trust me, I'm good at this."

"I know you are, but nobody's invincible."

We slipped through the streets, following the careful path Sola had marked out. "They've got as many cameras up as we do," she'd said. "but the last I checked, this was the least-covered route."

At the edge of the last block, Trini stepped inside a doorway, huddled up as small as she could.

I crouched down next to her. "I'll be out as quick as I can. You wait here. I can't be worried about you, too."

"So I get to do all the worrying," she teased, smiling bravely.

"Nope. Neither of us should be worried. In and out,

the old lady home to her grandkids. Then we use Sola's contacts to figure out what Mada's up to."

She gave a sharp nod. "It'll be worth it."

I didn't look behind me as I stepped away and tried to shove every thought of her from me.

But it didn't work.

Still, years of missions and training made spotting the first guard easy. I slid around him and he never noticed.

A shimmer in the night air caught my attention and I froze.

Infrared.

Likely a motion detector.

I turned and found another path, moving closer to the target building.

If I was as good as I claimed to be, surely I'd be able to get in and get out without having to strike a single blow.

That was always the optimal situation.

A second guard, a third, then I was into the building itself. Silent except for the heavy footsteps above me.

I counted, listening for differences in their gait.

Three guards on patrol upstairs.

Workable.

Whoever had taken Sola and Venac's grandmother had been smart.

Heat signatures indicated the room she was kept in was completely internal to the building.

No windows, no vents, no convenient balconies.

No easy way in.

Slowly I crept along the first floor, pausing and listening.

Still only the pacing of the guards.

I'd have to decide what to do with them when I got there.

Killing or even incapacitating them might mean risking their missing a check-in, which would raise the alarm as much as if I'd started a fire fight.

One of the guards was just a bit slower than the others. Matching their footfalls to my mental copy of the model Sola had made of the building, they walked a circuit of the hallways around the target's room.

And one of them was off pattern.

I crept up another level.

Listened.

Their paces held.

The slower guard was out of sync with the other two enough to give me a window to get in, and a longer one to get out.

Perfect.

Crouching low against the corridor wall, I listened, and counted.

Then lightly sprinted the rest of the way.

Silently sliding open the door, I slipped inside, then spun quickly to block a chair from crashing into my hip.

"Stop that!" I said in as low of a voice as I thought an elderly woman would be able to hear. "Your grandchildren sent me. Try not to make any noise, would you?"

The room was dark, but I could see her just fine. The same iron gray hair as Sola, but pulled into a tight bun. She had been tall once, but was now stooped. She didn't look injured, and from the way she'd swung that chair, I'd bet she'd given her kidnappers plenty of trouble.

Good for her.

Her eyes searched my darkened form, but couldn't make enough detail to see anything.

"How do I know that?" she whispered.

"Sola sent this with me." I held the trinket out towards her, then realized she wouldn't be able to see it. "Put your hand out."

She did and I dropped the token onto her palm, her fingers immediately tracing the pattern.

"Right then," she said sharply. "Get me out of here. These people are nitwits."

"It will be easier if you let me lead you," I suggested.

She scowled, but held out her left hand to take mine,

grip still tight on the token Sola had sent in her other hand.

The footsteps of the first, faster guard passed the door.

We waited.

The second faster guard passed, and as the step faded, I slid open the door.

"Now," I said and we slipped down the hall away from the room.

Until the old woman stumbled.

I swore under my breath.

"Are you injured?"

"No, you fool, you just move too fast."

But we'd lost our window.

The third guard rounded the corner.

"What are you doing out of your room, Mrs. Deleste?" he exclaimed, hurrying to the old woman's side. "These people aren't nice, you don't want to cross them."

Then he saw me. "Are you breaking her out? Can you take me?"

That... was unexpected.

"Why would I do that?"

"Of course not," the woman answered for me.

I glanced at her, warily. "We don't really have time for this, ma'am."

But she didn't stop. "You betrayed me, betrayed my family, and betrayed the quarter."

Each statement fell like a blow on the man, and as he shrank from the force of her words, she seemed to stand a little taller.

"You don't understand," he said. "They told me they'd kill my daughter if I didn't do as they said, cooperate. There's nowhere to send her where Mada couldn't reach."

This was Hosk, then.

The old woman's face didn't soften.

"If you had a problem, you should've come to the family. You know that." She nodded sharply. "But as a favor for past service, I'll make sure your daughter is taken care of."

She held out the black box, and too late I realized what was going to happen.

The bang of the hidden weapon shattered the quiet air.

Hosk's body slumped against the wall and the woman still scowled at him in annoyance. "Disloyalty must be punished."

"It could have waited till we were out of here, lady."

If the way in had been so easy it was almost boring, the way out wasn't going to be.

Not anymore.

Footsteps came pounding towards us.

Come on, come on, I thought, mentally spinning through the building's corridors and rooms.

Got it.

This way.

This time I didn't bother to politely wait for her.

This time, I tossed the old biddy over my shoulder and ran.

A right, a left, and another left, until we were in a large empty room with a small window looking over the street. I sat the woman down unceremoniously and started ripping panels from the floor.

"Young man, if you don't tell me what you're doing right this moment—"

Shoving the panels against the door, I layered as many as I could, then stacked the rest in front to hold them. "Saving your life," I snapped. "You can tell me I'm doing it wrong later."

Shots jolted against the jury-rigged door, but it held.

For now.

I turned to the window.

"You won't be getting out that way," she argued. "You've just trapped us here. That's blastproof plexi."

"That's what I'm hoping for," I muttered, then rammed my fingers into the wall at the side of the window.

Again, and again, until I'd made enough of an

opening that I could wedge my hands in, feel the edge of the window.

"Stand back," I snarled, and this time, she listened.

With a wrenching twist, I tore the window from the wall, leaving a gaping hole, then forced a final piece of the floor into a loop, cramming it on the edge of the plexi to form a makeshift handle.

"Hang on," I said, holding her to me with one arm, and holding the plexi over my head. "Time to go."

"Young man, put me down right nooo—"

The door shattered behind us just as I leaped through the newly made exit, holding the plexi over my head for cover.

Landing on the street level with a thump, plasma blasts rocked our improvised shield as I swung it around awkwardly to cover my back.

"Whoever sold them this stuff should be sued," I muttered.

Blastproof turned out to be more like blast-resistant.

With every impact, I could feel the plexi vibrate just a bit more.

It wouldn't take many more hits before it splintered.

I tore down the street, racing for Trini's hiding place.

But she wasn't hiding anymore, instead she was running to meet me.

Another blast hit the plexi so hard I almost stumbled.

I set the finally silent old woman down and pushed her into Trini's open arms.

"Go!" I shouted, and turned back to the fight.

TRINI

And we ran until my breath caught, until my lungs sobbed for air.

I locked my arm around the old woman's waist, half-carrying her along with me.

"Are you hurt?" I shouted over the sounds of lasers as we made our way down the street, trying to hug the storefronts to present a smaller target.

She didn't answer.

I risked stopping for a moment to look over at her.

As much as Venac and Sola valued her, they'd be upset if their beloved grandmother had taken damage while being rescued.

But I couldn't see anything wrong with her, other than a fine layer of dust covering her hair and clothes.

"He jumped," she finally answered. "He just jumped."

Ah. That would explain it.

"He does things like that," I said. It wasn't much of an explanation, but it was all we had time for.

Anything else I would've said was cut off as streams of men and women flowed out from the buildings between us and the enemy's hideout.

They lay down covering fire and one tall man turned to yell, "Get her back to the house!"

We hurried on, and with each step, I worried more.

Quinn wasn't alone in the battle anymore, but would they take care not to hit him?

Had Sola made it clear whose side he was on?

Another block closer to the house and Venac and Sola stood in the street, waiting for us.

As Venac embraced his grandmother in a bear hug, Sola spoke into a comm. "We've got her. Take the bastards apart."

"Do you mind—" My knees weakened slightly as my words were lost in another explosion. "Do you mind if we get inside?" I waved my arm vaguely over my head. "I'm not really used to all this. It's been a crazy couple of days and my brain hasn't caught up yet."

"With the company you keep, I'd assumed this would be a regular occurrence for you." Sola tilted her head to the side. "What's your regular job?"

"I'm a waitress," I said weakly. "At least I was. Now I'm not sure what I am, other than scared."

She laughed, and with a sweep of her arm, four more fighters surrounded us as we made our way back to their house.

Venac led his grandmother down the hall. "A long hot bath and you won't even remember the inconvenience."

"Nonsense, boy," she snapped. "Of course I will. Someone needs to bring in that traitor Hosk's daughter, though. I made him a promise and I mean to keep it."

I didn't know what they were talking about, but Venac laughed. "Thought you might want to take care of that personally. Come on, your room is all made up."

In the dining-room-turned war room, I sat, a mug of kaf going cold in my hands, untasted as I watched the screens.

But there was too much to make any sense of it.

Explosions and plasma blasts filled the air as each screen rotated through different views.

Until suddenly, there was silence.

"Where is he?" I whispered.

But there was no answer.

Long minutes stretched on, my chest burning until I forced myself to breathe regularly.

"Stop!" I shouted.

One of the screens had caught a glimpse of Quinn and, at my outburst, Sola froze it, keeping it locked on him as he strode away from the battleground.

My eyes searched over his body, but other than being bloodied and covered in scrapes, he seemed fine.

He'd get over those soon enough, I knew now.

I ran to the door, but Venac, returning from settling his grandmother in, caught me before I could reach it.

"He's not going to thank us if you get hit by a stray round after having gotten you home safe," he said. "Your man will be here soon enough."

And he was.

As he came into the room, I ran to him and he crushed me to his chest.

Warmth ran through me at his touch.

He was back, safe. For the moment, nothing could touch us.

After a long, wonderful moment, he grabbed my shoulders, fingers clenching tight. "What did you think you were doing?" His narrowed eyes ran over me, checking for injuries. "You were supposed to stay hidden, stay safe." His voice was a low growl, but nothing he did could scare me.

"I'm sorry, I couldn't help it."

He pulled me back to him, but this time in a gentle embrace. "It's over now."

"This part." I swallowed, forcing myself to remember that it wasn't over. Not at all.

He released me enough to turn and face Sola, keeping one arm wrapped tightly around my waist.

"You've got your grandmother back safe and sound," he said. "Your enemies are either dead or scattered. Nobody's going to be using that building for anything other than a construction site. Now we need some information in return." He flashed a tight grin. "Think of it as a favor."

"We know Mada Sommu is after me," I said. "But we don't know why. Surely, with all your contacts, you can find out something? People always talk eventually, right?"

Sola glanced up from the tablet she'd been working on, her expression grim. "I suspect in a few moments you'll be able to ask herself yourself." She threw the image from the tablet up to the largest of the wall screens.

A flitter slowly hovered down a street I didn't recognize, but could guess was somewhere in the Fourth Quarter.

Around it marched a squad of men, all dressed entirely in flat black, faces covered, hands gauntleted.

I shook, moving even closer to Quinn. "They're dressed just like the men that tried to take me from the Merry Stormcloud," I whispered. "Aren't they?" I looked up at him.

He nodded, jaw set.

"That's not good," Venac said. "The only ones that wear that uniform are Mada's personal guard."

"So that means…" I trailed off as Sola switched to a new camera further down the street and zoomed into the lightly tinted bubble covering the cabin of the flitter.

Another adjustment to the cameras, and suddenly we could see inside.

A driver with another guard to his side was in the front.

And in the back seat, the beautiful, cruel face of Mada, eyes fixed forward, small smile of triumph on her crimson lips.

But that wasn't what made me gasp.

Because of the angle, we could only see the top of the blaster, but it was enough to know that it was shoved into Risti's side.

Quinn's arms tightened around me as I struggled to break away.

"They're headed right here, I'd bet," he said flatly. "No point in meeting them halfway."

And he was right.

The flitter stopped in front of the house, the guards circled around it, then Mada dragged a pale and trembling Risti out behind her.

"I'd thought my boys would be able to leverage the local slumlords into handing you over," Mada said softly, her voice amplified so it rang through the house. "But that failed, so I thought I'd take care of it myself.

Trini Donnall, you have five minutes to surrender yourself before your friend dies."

"Don't even think about it," Quinn said sharply as I moaned in horror.

But Mada wasn't done. "After that, I'll fetch up your charming family from the south. You really don't have too many connections, do you? But I will find them all, and I will kill them all."

I was trembling now, not in fear but in anger.

"I'll at least let you decide, should I shoot your aunt and uncles first, or start with the children?"

Risti's eyes were closed, her face as pale as the moon. But her chin was high as she waited for whatever came.

"Four minutes," Mada said calmly, almost bored.

I turned to run my hand down Quinn's cheek. "You can't stop me. If you try to rescue her, Mada will kill my friend before you get halfway through her guards."

He started to argue, but I put my hand over his lips, silencing him.

"You know I'm right. I'd have to choose sometime." My throat tightened, and I had to force the words out.

"This is my choice."

Stunned, he dropped his hands, and I stepped away and walked out the door.

QUINN

I waited across the street from the cone shop, eyes peeled, gut burning.

Trini had been gone for twelve hours now.

And despite the rage howling through my blood, there was nothing I could do about it.

Yet.

People passed by, laughing and chatting as if nothing at all had changed.

But everything had.

Scouring the crowds around me, I was still startled when Torik popped up at my side.

"You look like you're in a fine mood." He glanced around. "Trini still saying goodbye to folks?" His face fell. "Don't tell me she decided to stay."

"Worse," I ground out. "Mada took her."

"What are we waiting for?" His eyes narrowed. "Or aren't you planning on getting her back?"

"I'll explain the plan when Mack — Killian — gets here. We have a stop to make first."

"Alright," Torik drawled out. "I'm always up for surprise errands. That's sort of how I got stuck on this rock."

"Before he gets here," I started, "there're a few things I should tell you about Mack. He's a little on edge these days."

Torik laughed, his eyes scanning the crowds just as mine were. "None of us have exactly been called happy-go-lucky individuals."

"True, but it's a little more than usual." I shrugged and gave up. He'd figure it out soon enough.

Torik smiled as Mack stomped down the middle of the street, heedless of the passersby or the stares he collected.

"Don't like this," he growled as he handed me a small parcel. "Zayda's by herself on the *Queen*. Can't be gone too long."

"Then let's make it fast so I can get my own mate back," I snapped.

Mack looked at Torik for the first time. "This is the guy we're here for? Good. Let's get going."

As I led the way back to the Fourth Quarter, Torik and Mack flanked me.

"Never seen so many people who refuse to acknowl-edge what's right in front of them," Torik commented. "I really hate this place."

Interesting, but right now, I didn't care. As soon as we got off the Boulevard, I started to run.

I wasn't interested in discretion now. It was nice, not having to pretend to care.

We were back in the Fourth Quarter in no time.

Everyone had been busy since Mada took Trini.

My quiet, cheerful lady had made a lot of friends over the years.

The crowd of involved parties was far too large to fit in Sola and Venac's house, so headquarters had been moved, temporarily at least, to Dr. Jaylan's warehouse. Nonna Deleste had taken over the remodeling.

If I was in a mood to be amused by anything, watching gang members hustle to clean, sweep, and reorganize at her direction might've done it.

Maybe it would be funny when I told Trini about it later.

If I got the chance.

"About time you were back," Sola said as she built up her model.

Rather, built it down.

Unwilling to spoil the skyline of her profitable vaca-tion paradise, Mada had built the headquarters for her corp deep underground.

Not even Sola's heat trackers had been able to build a reliable blueprint, but Risti and her friends had been able to fill in some of the blank spots.

"You'd be amazed at how much men talk when they're relaxed," she'd smirked.

"It'll be swarming with her thugs," Torik said, looming over the table. "Do we have a count yet?"

"You'll have a lot fewer to take care of once we get started with our end of things," Russar answered.

At his side was thin, dark Paulo. "I've got the shields prepped, whenever you're ready."

In theory, the plan was simple.

Risti and her co-workers would flood the Carnival, enticing the tourists and civilians back to the Boulevard with treats from the merchants. No doubt, they'd be able to lure most of the adults just with a finely placed cock of the hips.

Venac and Sola's people would take the Carnival attendees' places, some dressed like vacationers, some in caricatures of their regular clothing.

Once the Carnival was clear, the fun would start.

And the explosions.

"Security won't dare ignore so much damage, not in one of the most heavily trafficked areas of Rondi," Russar nodded. "They'll have to come out in full force."

Paulo grinned, eyes lit with mischief. "And once they're inside, they'll be trapped."

The force shields that kept the kiddies from running too far afield had been strengthened and adjusted, until only people wearing a new type of wristband would be able to pass through.

Our people.

"Don't know how many will be left in the headquarters, though," Venac said, rubbing his chin. "Sure you don't want us to send more fighters with you?"

"Not much of a plan. Tear it all apart. Kill everyone. Get the woman. Get out." Mack shrugged. "You'd just be in our way."

Venac blinked, and looked between the three of us. "Maybe you're right."

"He is," I said flatly. "Show us what you've got. How do we get in?"

Sola spun the model and overlaid a city map onto it. "Mada's smart. She's kept her building on a totally separate power grid and maintenance system from the city." Sola highlighted an access point. "As far as I can tell, this is the place where the city's maintenance shafts come closest to Mada's network. If you can get through the barrier, you'll end up in her system."

"We'd better get into place, then." I turned to head out, but was stopped by Nonna Deleste's scowl.

"Get that girlie back, you hear me?" She tossed a commlink at me. "She's a sweet little thing. Shouldn't be caught up in all this nonsense."

"I know," I agreed, my chest tight, and sealed the link to my skin.

As we took our position in the maintenance shaft, her words echoed in my mind.

Trini wasn't part of this world. Not a spy or a thief, not a hacker or fighter.

She was sweet and gentle. Kind.

No matter how I felt about her, I couldn't ask her to leave her family, to join a pack of mercenaries, always in the middle of chaos.

My mind sheared away from the logical conclusion of that thought, back onto the mission.

We didn't really need the commlink.

The vibrations from the first set of explosions rocked us, even this far underground

"Let's do this thing," Mack growled, and as one we started up the three powerful plasma drills, borrowed from some of Paulo's contacts.

Through the permasteel that held the city's massive ducts together.

Down through the rock that separated the systems.

The drills heated, running longer and hotter than they were designed for, but we weren't going to stop.

Finally, with a last crack of stone, we were through the exterior of the complex's shafts.

We were in.

The passageway was a tight fit, barely big enough

for a man to walk through. No cables or pipes ran through it, it was likely just for air circulation.

No matter. We'd use what we found.

We hunched over, our loping strides cramped by the space.

"If we get jumped here, it's going to be a mess," Mack growled.

"I'll try to leave you a few to play with," I called back.

"You're both idiots, do you know that?" Torik grunted. "Let's find a way out of this place."

Before long the shaft met another, larger one, and we took a moment to stretch.

"Bingo," Torik said, pointing to a bundle of cables. "That looks like what you wanted, right?"

"Exactly." I took the package Mack had handed me and clipped a gleaming silver block to the outermost of the cables. "You in there yet?"

Almost, Nixie chirped. *Give me just a minute, it's all tangly in here.*

I handed out commlinks to Torik and Mack while we waited.

Alrighty! I'll give you directions, and see if I can find your friend.

"It's not going to be 'if', Nixie," I insisted. "You will find her, and quickly."

You're really grouchy today, do you know that? Do you

need a nap? Eris always says Connor needs a nap when he's grouchy and the baby—

"Just find Trini."

Fine, she said. *Keep going straight, turn left at the third shaft.*

On we went, twisting and turning through the maintenance tunnels at Nixie's directions, getting ever closer to the heart of Mada's fortress.

"Any word on Trini yet?" I growled. "We've been down here for 10 minutes, somebody's gonna notice soon."

Probably not, Nixie answered. *I've been shutting off alarms as you passed them. And there's not a lot of people here anyway, really. It looks like you were right, most of her soldiers did leave to investigate those explosions.*

"That's good," I said as we took the next corner. "But that doesn't get me Trini."

Everything is encrypted differently here, she huffed.

"That's what you wanted, wasn't it?"

It was! I just thought I'd have time to play with it!

We ran farther.

Wait, stop!

We froze

I've caught her, but... For once the AI sounded unsure of herself.

"But what, Nixie?" Mack demanded.

I think bad things are happening, she said softly.

"Patch in the audio," I commanded. "Now."

Quinn, you won't be able to do anything till you get there, she argued. *Let me just give you directions, then you can help.*

"Send me the audio!"

Then my chest was torn open by the sound of Trini's screams.

"I told you, I don't know what you're talking about," she sobbed.

The high-pitched whining in the background stopped and I realized it was some sort of device.

Someone was torturing her.

"Get me there *now!*" But even as I barked out the words, I didn't know if we'd make it in time.

A soft, easy laugh. Mada. "Such a pity." A clank of metal. "You've been so lonely down here, haven't you? You'll be glad to know we've finally caught up with your partner."

Another turn, down another level.

Deeper into this hell hole, but still not close enough.

"Quinn?" Trini whimpered. "No. He's supposed to be gone."

"That merc you were with the other night?" Mada scoffed. "You'll have to try harder, dear. I saw through that little ploy immediately." Her voice rose as she called out. "Bring him in!"

"Hey, baby!"

My snarl echoed through the metal corridor.

Makkar.

"You could have just said you wanted to—hey, that hurts!"

"Good," I growled.

"He got Trini into this, somehow," I explained as we finally dropped out of the shafts and into the complex proper. The hallways were abandoned, dimly lit. It didn't matter. "And I'm going to kill him for it."

Makkar's screams were now echoing through the comms.

"You might not get a chance," Torik said. "Sounds like the lady holds a grudge."

"How much farther, Nixie?" I shouted.

Next hallway to the right, she's in a room at the very end, but there's a squad of...

"We see them," Torik growled. "Keep going, Quinn. We'll take care of these guys."

Springing forward, I leaped over the heads of the black-clad guards, landing squarely on one. Pushing off, I raced down the hall, ears ringing with Mack's laughter.

He always did love a good fight.

Pity those guys probably weren't going to be in any shape to give him one.

"Fine! Stop!" Makkar cried out. "I'll give it to you!"

"Good boy," Mada purred. "Where is my data?" The high-pitched whine started up again.

"Trini has it!" he shrieked.

My brain froze, even as I kept running.

After all this time, all those denials, had she been playing me for a fool all along?

And did it even matter?

No.

"What are you talking about?" Trini shouted. "I don't have anything from you!"

"Check under the skin on her left shoulder," he hurried to explain. "She didn't know about it, I used a mini-injector to plant it on her, to buy me some time."

"Not as dumb as you look," Mada answered. "Let's take a look, shall we?"

And finally, I was at the door.

TRINI

Even with my blurry vision, I could see the terror on Makkar's face.

It was easy to recognize.

For the last while, it was the only thing I'd felt myself.

He was strapped to another one of these damn chairs, Mada standing over him with one of her endless, bloody toys, green silk blouse shot through with bronze threads, and black flowy pants looking more like she was on the way to a party instead of amusing herself in a makeshift torture chamber.

"Check her arm, I swear you'll find it there," he shrieked.

But she didn't move. Not yet.

I'd realized she enjoyed letting things drag out.

Slowly bringing you to the breaking point.

"Well, maybe I will." Casually, she stuck the knife into the padding of the chair, barely missing the side of his face, then walked towards me. "It's not like you're going anywhere anyway."

My throat was dry from screaming.

But I had to try.

"If I have a chip, a whatever this is about, I didn't know," I pleaded.

"Well, at this point I'm not sure if it matters much."

She reached for a different slim blade, then the door flew open.

"Quinn!" I tried to shout, but it came out as more of a rusty croak.

Oh no, he couldn't be here.

She'd kill him.

She'd kill him in front of me, then I really would be dead in every way that mattered.

But still, it was so good to see him.

His face grew grim as he took in the scene before him.

"Back. Away. Slowly."

"Really?" Mada snapped. "You think you're giving orders in my base?" She lunged forward and flicked the knife across my arm.

I bit my lip to keep from crying out, but it didn't matter.

Quinn had seen the blood.

"I hadn't decided about killing you before," Quinn growled. "I have now."

"You and what army?" she said and, with the snap of her fingers, the far door opened and the room filled with her guards, and even though I should have been numb to them by now, I still flinched back in my bonds.

From behind Quinn, two more giant shapes appeared.

Torik and a feral-looking stranger.

The stranger tossed one of the matte black masks into the center of the floor, a crimson trail splattering behind it.

"I expect we're all the army it's going to take," Torik said.

The swarm of guards surged forward as Mada stepped behind their defensive line.

Then the chaos began.

I tried to huddle down in the chair, but the bonds were too tight for me to move.

In a moment, Quinn was at my side, ripping through the restraints, while the other two engaged Mada's guards.

"Oh sweetheart," he said as he took in the damage

Mada had done. "We're going to get you out of here, get you to a doctor."

I nodded, trying to keep the tears from welling in my eyes.

"I didn't know about the chip," I whispered. It seemed important to tell him that.

"It doesn't even matter," he said. "But I believe you." He lifted me gently and placed me by the wall to the side of the door.

"There's no place with good cover in here," he said, hand hovering a fraction of an inch from my cheek. "Stay low, we'll clean this up in a few minutes."

If anyone else had said that, I would've laughed.

If it didn't hurt so much.

There must've been thirty of Mada's personal guards, all in their black armor, all armed with blasters.

But Torik and the stranger had already made a sizable dent in their number. Plasma blasts were knocked wild and high as Torik picked up one of the guards and threw him full force into a cluster of his brethren.

"I don't expect I'll be going anywhere," I said.

"Good. We've got a lot to talk about." He pressed a kiss to the top of my head, then left to join the fight.

Makkar's shrieks kept breaking through the clatter and sizzle of the battle. "Don't leave me here! Someone, anyone, help me!"

I stayed curled in my little ball, wrists over my ears, hands laced over the back of my neck.

I'd read somewhere about that being the safest position to take...but maybe that was for earthquakes. Or shuttle crashes.

Who was I kidding? I've never read anything that was helpful about anything like this.

A thud shook me as another one of the guards was flung into the wall above me and slid down into a boneless pile.

"Sorry about that, Trini!" the stranger called out. "I'm Mack!" and dove back into the melee.

Well. That was sort of an introduction. I could only assume this was another of Quinn's brothers. No one else could possibly look like that.

Move like that.

And Makkar kept screaming.

He must be terrified.

I, at least, had people here to fight for me.

And he's the one who got me into this, I reminded myself.

But he was Russar's brother, and if I left him strapped in that chair, he was going to get killed, even if it was by mistake.

Slowly, I forced myself to uncurl and peek around the room.

Few of Mada's guards still stood. They formed a

tight cluster, taking random shots at the three men who moved faster than anything I'd ever seen.

Quinn and his brothers leaped from wall to ceiling and back again, dodging the shots with ease, then reaching out to snatch one hapless guard at a time out of their safe huddle.

Taking a deep breath, I crawled around the body of the guard Mack had thrown, further along the wall until I was almost parallel with the chair Makkar was strapped into.

His eyes were wide and unseeing. He'd stopped yelling, just muttering incoherently in terror.

"Be quiet," I whispered, then put my hand over my own mouth.

Crawling over the still forms of fallen guards, I picked my way across the room to his chair.

I risked a glance over to where the fighting still dragged on.

Maybe I should wait for Quinn.

But the longer Makkar was out in the open like this, the higher the chances one of those stray blasts would hit him.

Or me.

Then let's make it quick, Trini, I thought, and kicked myself into motion.

I rose to my knees and tried to unfasten the straps that held his wrists to the chair.

"Stop struggling," I whispered.

"Get me out get me out get me out get me out"

"I can't believe I ever dated you, even for just a month."

But I couldn't loosen the thick straps.

Finally, I grabbed the knife Mada had driven into the chair.

"You really need to be still," I hissed.

I hunched back down on the floor, sawing through the straps that bound his ankles. "If you kick me," I muttered as the sharp blade eventually worked through one, then the other, restraint, "I'm going to leave you here."

I glanced across the room again.

There were fewer guards now, but they were still holding out.

I took a deep breath and started working on Makkar's right wrist.

"Trini, I promise that..." he started whining.

"Shut up," I snapped, and kept working.

Just as I cut through the last strands of the restraint, something caught the corner of my eye.

I froze, turned my head just enough so I could see, then bit my lip to keep from gasping.

Almost directly behind us, a panel slowly slid open in the opposite wall, revealing a hidden passage.

Mada stood there, narrowed eyes the only sign of her displeasure as she raised a blaster shoulder high.

Straight at Quinn's back.

My heart caught.

There was no way he could hear me over the sounds of the battle.

Then I threw the knife.

QUINN

I dropped the last of the guards, then spun as a glint of silver caught my eye.

Mada stood against the far wall, holding a blaster, and with a knife quivering in her shoulder.

She swung the blaster towards the middle of the room.

Towards Trini.

Trini, who was standing by the chair the idiot was strapped into, instead of safe where I'd left her.

Then a final plasma blast shattered the air and Mada crumpled, a bloom of crimson spreading over her chest.

"I got her! I got her!"

Torik strode over to Makkar and kicked the blaster out of his hand.

Huh. It was almost impressive how far terror and desperation could encourage a man.

One hand still tied to the chair, Makkar had managed to fling himself far enough out to snag a blaster from one of the dead guards.

Surely, he was protecting himself, not Trini.

But he'd just earned himself a slight reprieve for getting her into this.

Very slight.

I ran over to Trini and she collapsed against me, shaking, eyes wide and frantic. "I didn't kill her, did I?"

"No, honey, it wasn't you." I stroked her cheek. "You saved me, though."

"Just as well Mada's dead, though," Torik said, stooping over the body. "There's not exactly much in the way of justice outside of the corporations here. Anything Mada did was legal."

"Then I guess we should be leaving?" Mack suggested, looking around the destruction of the room.

I scooped Trini into my arms, the smell of her blood making me more than a little crazy, but rage and anger weren't what she needed right now.

"Nixie," I commanded. "Plot me the fastest way out of this place."

You got it, boss.

Whether there were no more guards in the complex, Nixie had sealed them all out of our way, or they'd simply gotten smart, we didn't run into any more trouble.

An express elevator took us the rest of the way out in mere minutes, opening into a perfectly normal-looking shop, filled with high-end handbags and scarves and wispy things I assumed were meant to be clothing.

Nixie must've been busy because, instead of the expected shoppers, we had a welcoming committee of our own.

"Bring her here," Jaylan snapped, pointing to a table he'd rigged with a portable scanner and other bits of medtech I didn't recognize. "Put her down and let me work."

I couldn't bring myself to let her go, but lowered her onto the table, keeping one arm around her shoulders. "She's been quiet this whole time." I brushed the sweat-dampened hair out of her face. "I don't like it. I don't know what that bitch did to her down there."

"If you'd get out of my way," Jaylan pushed me back a half-step, "then I could find out what's going on. Terrible patients, all of you." He pushed a hypo against her upper arm and the last bit of tension eased from her frame.

"What was that?" I barked. "What did you give her?"

He rolled his eyes. "Deadly poison. What did you think?" I started to growl, and he quickly explained.

"General booster. Used to give them to the fighters all the time when they'd come out of the pit. Has a bit of everything needed to encourage the healing process to begin as quickly as possible, while I sort out the specifics of the problem."

He ran a scanner slowly over her and the healing wand followed.

"Let's get this out of her now." He skillfully applied a set of micro-tweezers to her shoulder, extracting a tiny metallic oval. "That must be what all the fuss was about."

I slipped it into my pocket as Russar and Risti pushed their way through the crowd. Risti stroked the back of Trini's hand, tears smudging her glittering eye makeup.

"I'll never forgive myself. I never wanted her to come out. She should have stayed in where it was safe."

Russar snorted. "Not our girl, not when a friend was in danger."

Jaylan finally put down the scanner and gave a sigh that told me he'd been just as worried as I was, even if he wouldn't admit it. "All the damage is superficial. The wand should help with the regeneration, close up the rest of those cuts. The booster will take care of it." He patted my arm. "She'll be fine."

"Physically," Russar said grimly.

"Hush," Risti insisted. "When this is over, we're

going to go get cones and win all the prizes and she's never going to think about any of this again. I won't let her."

"Great, she's fine," came a whine from behind us. "Who's going to take a look at me? I'm the hero here, anyway!"

"The hero." Russar turned slowly away from Trini's side to stare blankly at his little brother, still squirming in Torik's grasp.

"You and your big game plans. Your fancy schemes. Gonna get rich one day, some way." He stalked towards Makkar, who cringed back, but couldn't escape from Torik. "You stole from Mada. You got Trini involved. You led the guards right to our home, MY HOME, without ever thinking of warning us." He grabbed Makkar by the shoulders and held him up at arms' length, feet dangling above the floor. "You're not a hero, never will be. You're a scheming weasel who brings other people down into his muck."

Risti stepped to Russar's side, Paulo moved to the other. The three made a wall, blocking Makkar from Trini, from the rest of us.

"I don't have a little brother anymore," Russar declared, shaking Makkar with every word. "Not one that would risk hurting our little sister like this."

Russar flung Makkar away, and I didn't look to see where the little bastard scrambled off to.

I didn't care, as long as I never saw his face again.

Slowly, steadily, the color was coming back to Trini's face, the fine razor cuts almost totally sealing.

Jaylan ran the wand over the worst of them again and again, until nothing more than fine lines remained. The bruising was still discolored, but the swelling had receded entirely.

Trini moaned softly, and for a moment, I wished Mada was still alive, so I could kill her myself.

"Don't you have a tank or something, we could put her in?" I said. "Just for a week or two, just to finish healing up?"

Jaylan tilted his head to the side and Torik kicked my ankle.

"They don't do that here." He raised his eyebrows significantly. "Or anywhere really, right?"

Stupid rules.

It was just as well. Two weeks waiting for her to come out, not being sure how she was doing, would probably kill me.

So instead, I just waited, watching the bruises fade to just a slight memory.

Trini's eyelids fluttered open, revealing those gorgeous hazel irises that I could get lost in.

"Hey there," I said softly. "How are you doing?"

"I think I need a cleaning tube," she answered. "Did we win?"

"You won everything with that throw, love." She smiled, and it was the most amazing thing I'd ever seen. "We'll have to go back to the Carnival soon. You'll clean them out of all the ugly dolls."

I meant to kiss her softly, but when she wound her arms around my neck and pulled me closer, I couldn't help it.

To come so close to losing her.

To know that I'd have to leave her to keep her safe.

It was weak of me, but I couldn't resist the taste of her, the feel of her lips against mine.

Only the cheers and whistles of the watching crowd made me pull away.

Trini's cheeks were flushed.

"I guess you're feeling better?"

"We could go home now," she answered. "Think my room is clean yet?"

"Nonsense," Nonna Deleste pushed her way through the crowd. "You're coming back to our house. I've got dinner cooking." She nodded at me sharply. "I knew perfectly well your man would get you out of there."

I lifted Trini back into my arms and she nestled against my chest. "I'm gonna take another nap for a bit, okay?"

"Whatever you want," I promised. Nonna Deleste led the procession back toward the Fourth Quarter, and for once, the tourists seemed to have a notion that something different, something out of the ordinary to their regular rounds of pleasure, was taking place.

Mack appeared by my side. "Gotta get back to Zayda and the *Queen*," he muttered. "We'll be ready to bounce out, just say the word." He glanced at Trini, and the wildness in his eyes softened just a bit. "Whenever she's ready."

A terrible thought struck me. "Did we leave Nixie's extension looped into Mada's network?"

He grinned and tapped the commlink behind his ear. "She's been copying files like a little demon. I think you're forgiven for not bringing her along in the first place."

Well. That would be interesting.

And not my problem.

Mack faded away, and Torik took his place.

"You've been here longer, kept your eye on things. Who do you think is going to try to take Mada's place?" I asked. "Surely she's got some sort of corporate successor."

"Information on that chip might let us know," he answered. "But there's no reason the people here would have to stick with her plans. There might be enough there for them to hold the planet as their own corp."

"Maybe," I admitted, only vaguely interested. We'd reached the edge of the quarter, and the streets were filled with Venac and Sola's fighters, some battered and ragged, but all looking like they'd had a hell of a party. "The one thing that's still bothering me is the off-world buyer."

"Who?" Torik answered, as we approached the Deleste house. Nonna most certainly had been cooking, and it smelled delicious.

"In the recording we found of Mada, where she discovered Makkar had stolen the files. She speculated that he'd found an off-world buyer, someone from another corp. I don't want some other outfit sweeping down here before these people have a chance to get organized."

"Ah." Torik scratched his head. "I don't know if you need to worry about that too much."

I paused as a flood of people passed us by. "Why not?"

"I was the buyer for the chip," Torik admitted with a shrug. "I've been stuck here for years, couldn't figure a way to get out, couldn't find a way to make things any less screwed up. Then that idiot posted that he had a cache of her personal files."

There weren't any words.

I just glared at him.

"What?" Torik threw his hands up into the air. "I don't have your skills with computers. If I was going to get any intel, it was going to have to be an inside job."

He grinned broadly as he opened the door for me. "I just wasn't willing to get as far inside as that idiot did."

Trini woke up as we entered. "You can let me down now, promise."

Reluctantly, I set her on her feet, watching carefully for any wobbling. Risti grabbed her hand. "Come on, let's get you cleaned up. I grabbed a few things."

"Of course you did," Trini laughed as they went upstairs.

I itched to follow them, but there were other things to do, and if Trini had wanted me, she'd have said so.

"Give me a hand with this, will you?" Venac hollered down the hallway.

Entering the war room, I found him staring at the screens and tablets that littered every surface.

"We haven't served dinner in here for years," he muttered. "But if I mess with Sola's organization of her stuff, she'll kill me just as fast as Nonna."

"That is a problem," I agreed. "Where is she, anyway?"

"Helping in the kitchen. Russar's back there with them, so I thought I'd take the easy job. I wasn't thinking at all," he moaned.

"Right, then, let's look for another room to put this all in," I offered.

By the time the war room had been turned back into

a dining room and enough chairs had been found for everyone, Trini and Risti were coming back downstairs.

Sola grabbed the dish I was carrying before I dropped it. "You look like you've been hit by a plasma bolt," she muttered, but I didn't hear anything else she said.

Whether the healing wand had finished the job, or Risti had applied some magical creams, Trini simply glowed. I'd never imagined rust to be something attractive, but the reddish brown dress that wrapped her figure was perfect.

She was perfect.

And it was going to kill me to leave her.

TRINI

Dinner was nothing short of amazing.

Like the kind of big, extravagant family dinner you hear about, a crowd of people laughing and talking over each other.

Maybe it was a little different than what other people had in mind, but it was exactly what I wanted.

Russar loomed over one end of the table, talking about the old days with Venac. So many stories I'd never heard!

Throughout the evening, he hadn't said a word about Makkar.

No one had.

I felt guilty about it, but honestly, I was glad he was gone. Hopefully, he was out of our lives forever.

Sola and Risti had bonded over enhancements and were now moving the silverware around, arguing about strategy and tactics. I had a feeling there were going to be some changes at Momma Deese's soon.

Paulo and Dr. Jaylan were deep in a discussion about modifying the medscanners, tweaking them to be even more sensitive.

"That's a terrible, wonderful idea," Nonna Desleste cackled. "You're a terrible, wonderful man. I wish I'd met you a few decades ago." Either Nonna Deleste had Torik wrapped around her little finger, or maybe it was the other way around. Either way, I didn't want to know what they were planning.

Laughter and the sound of everyone talking over each other filled the room.

Only Quinn was reserved, remote.

Every time I looked up, he was watching me, but his eyes slid away, refusing to meet mine.

Finally, I couldn't take it anymore and pushed away my plate before Nonna had a chance to load it with a third helping of layered pasta and vegetables.

"It was wonderful," I complimented her, patting my tummy. "And you're right, you can taste the difference with real vegetables." I scooted my chair back, and Quinn leaped to his feet, everyone watching me as if I might fall apart at any moment.

"I'm a little tired again," I announced. "Quinn, will you come with me for a minute?"

"You get a good night's sleep, girlie," Nonna patted my hand.

"Or not," Risti chimed in.

Quinn followed me upstairs, still silent, his presence filling the air between us , by the time I reached the door of our room, I wanted to scream.

I stood by the door, waiting for him to enter.

He paused, obviously uneasy.

And I'd had it.

"Really?" I snapped.

He blinked, startled, and a bitter smile twisted my lips.

Finally, something that broke through that damn calm.

Carefully, quietly, I closed the door behind him, and watched him stand by the bed, looking at the dresser, the lamp.

Anywhere but me.

"Why are you so angry with me?" I asked, the crack in my voice nearly betraying me.

"What?" He shook his head. "I'm not angry with you."

I leaned against the door. "Then what is all this about? You won't talk to me, won't look at me." I crossed my arms, hugging my gut. "You've got a funny way of not being angry."

He paced back and forth in the tiny room, three steps one way, three steps the other.

Back and forth.

Again, and again, the muscle in his jaw twitching.

"You went to help that bastard instead of staying safe!" he finally exploded. "You could have been killed!"

"Because I didn't want a friend — no, he's not a friend, but the brother of a friend to get shot by mistake!" I shouted back. A crazy thought struck me. "Are you jealous? Of Makkar?"

"What? Of that idiot? Of course not." He stepped towards me, held out a hand. "I'm angry that you always put everyone else first. I'm angry that you could have lost your life for his, and it's not a fair trade, not by a long shot."

"Nothing about this world is fair," I snapped. "And everyone is important, even people I don't like."

With one quick stride, he closed the distance between us.

"No," he cried, grabbing my shoulders. "Not everyone is important. Not to me. Only you."

Oh. A flutter started in my belly, a flicker of hope.

"Which is why I have to leave. And you have to stay here."

What?

"Who the hell are you to tell me what I'm going to do?" I shouted, twisting to break away from his grasp.

"I'm the man who loves you," he yelled back, his eyes wild. "I'm the one who knows what it's like in my world. It's dirty and ugly and dangerous."

"And that's acceptable for you, but not me?" I pushed at his broad chest, but he was as immovable as stone. "Did you forget it was people from my world that nearly got me killed?"

"No! How am I ever going to forget what you looked like when I finally got to you?" his voice broke. "Void, Trini, you were so hurt…"

Slowly, I ran my hands up his chest and cupped his face. "But I'm not hurt now," I whispered. "And by the way, I love you, too. Stop trying to run away from me, got it?"

He didn't move, didn't so much as breathe as his eyes searched mine.

Pushing up on my toes, I pressed my lips against his, darting my tongue out to tease the seam of his mouth.

He groaned, pulling me against him. "You make me crazy," he growled. "I can't think straight. I just want you. I know I should leave you, but I need you too much."

"Then show me," I insisted.

No sooner had the words left my lips than he ripped the dress off me.

I shrieked. "Risti's going to be so pissed."

"I'll find a way to make it up to her." He nibbled down the side of my neck. "I'll get her another one." His hand cupped the back of my head, fingers knotted in my hair. "Six of them. I don't care."

I reached for him, but he swiftly pushed my arms behind me, holding both my wrists gently with one strong hand.

"I don't even like sweets," he muttered as he resumed kissing his way down my chest, leaning me back till my breasts were level with his mouth. "But I can't resist you."

With a swirl of his tongue, he brought my tight nipple into his mouth, sucking and nipping at it, then switching his attention to the other while his hand moved up to knead and squeeze my whole aching breast.

"Quinn," I begged, head thrown back as I squirmed in his tight hold. "I need you."

He broke away from teasing me, a wicked grin of delight clear on his face. "Oh yes, Trini," he crooned, the deep rumble sending shivers through me, stoking the fire in my veins to an inferno. "I'll give you everything you need. Everything you want. And more."

So fast my breath caught in my throat, he released my wrists, spun me around, and pushed my back until I folded at the hips, my hands braced on the mattress.

"Fearless, beautiful, Trini," he said, and ran his hands down my sides, down my legs, then back up again, one hand cupping my dripping mound as the other lightly pinched and rolled the tight buds of my nipples.

The broad head of his cock paused as he slipped it between my slick folds, giving me a chance to get accustomed to his girth, then with one devastating thrust, he was in me.

"I will never let you go," he said as he pounded into me, his fingers at my hips pulling me back harder against him. "Never try to leave me again."

His teeth nipped into my shoulder, the sharp sensation startling me, and I bucked against him, the combination of sensations as he thrust against me, his fingers swirling against my clit, his chest covering my back, taking my breath.

He claimed me completely, and I shattered, lost everything.

Demolished and rebuilt and destroyed again.

Utterly his.

And I knew without any doubts, he was utterly mine.

———

"You're lucky Sola's clothes fit me well enough," I teased Quinn in the morning as I tugged on a shirt that was just a bit too tight. "Good thing we're heading home for me to pack."

"It was a nice dress," he admitted, eyes glazing just a bit. "I'm looking forward to seeing what else you have in your wardrobe."

"So you can rip it off me?" I leaned against him, content just to have him near, just for a moment. "We're going to have to talk about that."

"Talk all you want." He slung our bags over his shoulder and held the door open for me. "We'll just have to get you more clothing. You're far too tempting."

The house was quiet when we went downstairs.

"Where do you think everyone is?" I whispered. "Still sleeping?"

"Humph," Nonna Deleste grumbled as she bustled out of the kitchen, Torik carrying a tray of pastries behind her. "More like they haven't gone to bed yet. I told them you can't develop a solid strategy for taking over a planet when you're sleepy, but they didn't listen. Kids these days!"

Quinn handed me a pastry without even asking, fastidiously brushing the excess sugar off his fingers when he thought I wasn't looking.

True love.

Torik shrugged. "There's a vacuum of power, now that Mada's gone. If they move fast enough, they'll have something in place before another corp attempts a takeover."

"You'll want this then," Quinn tossed him a tiny silver fleck, almost too small to see.

My stomach clenched. The damn data chip that had caused all this mess.

Torik snatched it midair and pocketed it. "It'll help, especially since your AI has had all night to play in Mada's system. She's pretty happy."

"That'll be a nice change," Quinn said. "Don't tell her I said so, but she's actually pretty helpful. Even when she's too curious for her own good or anyone else's."

After hugging Nonna goodbye, we headed out.

With every block that passed, I felt like I was saying goodbye.

"We'll come back, right?" I asked as we strolled back to the Boulevard, my fingers laced tightly with Quinn's. I was ready for adventure, ready to go with him.

But maybe I wasn't quite ready to leave forever.

Rondi never changed. Visitors swarmed the streets at all hours, shops glistened with every sort of pleasure.

But I knew that underneath the glitter, everything was different now.

"Of course," he answered. "Now that we've established contact with Heladae, I doubt the Emperor is going to want to let his foothold in the Areitis Sector go again." He squeezed my hand. "Maybe we should have him make you the official ambassador."

"Wouldn't that be fun to explain to my aunt!" I laughed, then stumbled as my brain caught up with my words. "Oh, Void! How am I going to explain any of this to them?"

Quinn moved to place one hand under my elbow as we kept walking. Good thing, since my mind was still stuttering, trying to wrap the last few days up into anything that made sense.

"How often do you usually see them?"

"I try to get down every few months." I did a quick count. "I'm not due for a visit for about six weeks, maybe seven."

"Easy enough," he said as he held open the door at the Merry Stormcloud. "That's plenty of time to come up with a cover story." He winked. "Or even some of the truth."

Ondar and Feevo had been busy. Hopefully, busy enough to have earned them a break on their tabs.

The broken furniture from the attack had been cleared away and replaced. One of Risti's friends danced at the front of the bar and gave a little wave as we passed by, managing to make it look like part of her routine.

"I see Russar didn't waste any time getting back in business," Quinn commented as we rounded the long U of the bar.

"Mada may be gone," I shrugged, "but he's still got to make a profit. Everyone here does."

A loud bang from the very back caught my attention. "What's going on here?" I hurried over, ready to break it up.

But it was Russar, thumping his fist on the table. "Why couldn't we re-incorporate as a workers-owned cooperative?" he argued.

Venac snorted. "You really think people are ready to just start self-governing after being under a corp's thumb for all these years?"

"Nothing says we can't give it a chance." Sola took a shot of trakko. From the dirty glasses stacked at her elbow, it didn't look like it was her first, but her voice was as clear as ever. "We just make sure we're the majority stakeholders so we can reconfigure later."

"Brilliant and evil," Risti exclaimed, leaning over to kiss Sola soundly. "I didn't have a chance."

Torik clapped Quinn on the shoulder as he made his way to the table. "I think I'm going to stay here for a bit. Sounds like it should be fun."

"Not happening," Quinn protested, grabbing Torik's arm. "You sent a distress call. We're here. Mission is over. You're coming home."

"Take it easy." Torik pulled away, snagging the chair next to Russar. "I've already told Mack, but you were a little occupied. I've got it on the very best authority that there's a spanking new ship that suddenly doesn't have an owner. And your helpful little AI has already loaded up the coordinates for the new HQ." He rocked back in the chair. "Orem Station, huh? Sounds interesting."

Quinn was still sputtering when I led him upstairs.

EPILOGUE: TRINI

In the end, there wasn't as much to pack as I'd expected.

A few favorite clothes, a holocube with pictures of my family.

A commtab.

And I was ready.

"Want to hit the Carnival?" Quinn asked. "Maybe go get some cones?"

I shook my head. "Too excited to eat," I explained. "I'll just look forward to it for when we come visit."

He pulled me into his broad chest, nuzzling at my hair. "I'll even try a new flavor. With sprinkles."

"I can't let you suffer with just plain, boring vanilla," I explained, wrapping my arms around his waist and turning my face up to watch his, still amazed that this glorious, mysterious, wonderful person was mine.

My future.

My everything.

He smiled, his steely eyes bright with amusement. "I'll show you plain and boring."

"No!" I laughed, scrambling away as he twisted us onto the bed. "You said your friends are waiting. We'll never get out of here at that rate!"

"True." He grabbed the bags and held a hand out to help me up. "I can wait until we're back on Orem."

"Seriously?" I pouted. "If I'd thought we were going to have to be good until we were on the other side of the galaxy, I might have given you a different answer."

Smug bastard just grinned.

Back downstairs, Russar smothered me in hugs until Risti pulled me away. "You can't tell me they don't have good comms where you're going," she insisted. "I expect to hear from you regularly, or we'll have to come looking." She narrowed her eyes at Quinn. "And I'll know who to blame."

"WHERE ARE WE GOING?" I asked as Quinn led me down the Boulevard, down to the sea-wall.

"We never did take a walk on the beach," he said, but

he eyed the water warily, as if expecting monsters to come for us.

"You could just tell me you want it to be a surprise," I argued as we made our way down the narrow steps to the sand. "But fine, be difficult. I like the beach." I ran to the edge of the water, let the waves chase me, as I had so many times before.

What would it be like, living on a space station? No sun, no beach…

"Having second thoughts?" Quinn had wandered further down the strand, almost to a rocky cove that cut into the shore line, a hidden little pocket I'd snuck into for picnics more than once.

"Nope!" I hurried to catch up. "Just getting some splashing time in."

He caught me as I ran past, almost into the cove. "We should wait back here." He frowned and pulled me back. "Maybe a little further away."

"Why?"

And then a sleek silver ship appeared in the air in front of us.

By the time it landed and the side hatch slid open, my breathing was almost back to normal.

Almost.

A beautiful woman, a long dark braid tossed over her shoulder, hopped out. "Calm down, it's just for a minute!" she called over her shoulder.

Running towards us, she hugged Quinn, then reached for me.

"Sorry, it's just exciting to meet you," she explained. "I'm Zayda, Mack's mate. Ready to go?"

Mack filled the doorway, obviously ready to rush out and crush anything that threatened his tiny mate. But his glower turned to adoration when Zayda swung back up to the hatch and pecked him on the cheek.

"We'll perch in the back," she announced. "More room for the two of you up front."

As she disappeared into the ship, I thought of how Mack looked at her.

As if she was the center of his entire world.

Quinn helped me into the ship and stowed the bags into a tiny cargo hold beneath the floor. "You'll be alright?" he asked.

He had the same look on his face that Mack did.

In love. Happy.

I bounced up to kiss him, just to watch him smile.

"Better than alright. Perfect."

"ARE you sure he's eating enough?"

I'd thought Nonna Deleste was intense.

That was before I met Doc. And Granny Z.

And all of the other amazing, somewhat over-whelming, members of Quinn's family.

"Those gorin," Doc continued without waiting for an answer. "I wonder if they have enough fat on them to keep his calorie count up. You'd be amazed at how much these boys need to keep going."

"Um, well," I stuttered, not entirely certain how to calculate how much fat had been on one of those murderous monsters. "Torik didn't look like he was going hungry." I took another sip of my drink.

Not trakko, but interesting. And maybe I could talk Torik into buying a few cases before he came home.

"Mind if I cut in, Doc?" Quinn asked with a casual kiss to the top of her head. "My lady still has lots of sights to see."

She smiled and suddenly the fierce scientist was replaced by a fond mother.

Or creator.

Something like that.

"You get settled in, dear. I want to go talk to Ronan." She smiled, and I pulled back a bit. Just a bit. "Maybe it's time to plan a little strike on that sector, before that busybody Vandalar gets involved."

Quinn's eyelid twitched, but all he said was, "As soon as you can drag him away from Nadira, feel free."

"Nonsense, with her connections, she'll be a great help in the campaign. And I know she'll be curious about that Dr. Jaylan when he arrives...So many projects!"

Quinn whirled me away to the balcony of the apartment.

Nadira had insisted on hosting the party. "Just a small welcome to the family," she had said.

Her smile was warm, but I was still scrambling to remember who everyone was.

She and Ronan shared an apartment in one of the larger residential hives. Near the top of the building, a balcony looked out over the busy streets below.

Quinn wrapped me in his arms and I buried my face against his chest.

"I don't want to see any other sights," I muttered. "Not for a little bit."

"We're not going anywhere," he promised. "I just figured you could use a rescue."

"It's not that she isn't nice," I hastened to explain.

He laughed. "Nobody's ever called Doc nice."

"But she is," I argued. "Everyone is. They're just a little overwhelming." Heat warmed my cheeks. "And honestly, a little intimidating. I about died when Kara casually mentioned that Zayda used to be a spy. Everybody seems so talented. Special."

I pulled away, staring out over the city.

"Hey," Quinn said, sliding his hands around my waist

from behind. "They each have their talents, but so do you." His arms tightened around me. "I've never met anyone who people like as much as they do you. Never met anyone who liked people so much, cared about them."

I let out a huff. "That's not really a talent."

"Have you met my family? We may be many things, but likable isn't really top of the list."

Leaning back into his solid comfort, my last worry broke free and found a voice. "But what am I going to do here?"

"Whatever you want." He turned me slowly to meet his gaze. "What do you want to do, more than anything?"

"I don't know," I admitted.

And maybe that was just as scary.

A future wide open, full of possibilities.

I looked out over the station again.

People went about their business, worked for their dreams.

Somehow able to not even think about the fact that they floated in the vacuum of space.

They were tethered by something else. By their families.

The lives they'd built here.

And maybe, if they were lucky, by love.

"Whatever you want to do, we'll make it happen."

His lips brushed mine again, filled with promise, filled with our future. "Together."

Next up? Hakon finally gets his story!

In the war between love and honor, can anyone win?

Determined to restore her family's honor, Yasmin has no time for romance. Certainly not when she's embedded on a rival corp's space station for a bit of industrial espionage.

But her mission is blown when the station falls under attack.

Rescued by a handsome stranger with secrets of his own, they crash on a desert planet.

She can she trust him long enough to survive?

And can love be more important than honor?

Forged is the tenth science fiction romance novel in The Star Breed series. No cliffhangers, no cheating, HEA guaranteed!

Click to preorder now!

PLEASE DON'T FORGET TO LEAVE A REVIEW!

Readers rely on your opinions, and your review can help others decide on what books they read. Make sure your opinion is heard and leave a review where you purchased this book!

Don't miss a new release! You can sign up for release alerts at both Amazon and Bookbub:
bookbub.com/authors/elin-wyn
amazon.com/author/elinwyn

For a free short story, opportunities for advance review copies, release news and the occasional cat picture, please join the newsletter!
https://elinwynbooks.com/newsletter-signup/

And don't forget the Facebook group, where I post sneak peeks of chapters and covers!

https://www.facebook.com/groups/ElinWyn/

NEED TO CATCH UP WITH THE STAR BREED?

Given: Star Breed Book One

When a renegade thief and a genetically enhanced mercenary collide, space gets a whole lot hotter!

Thief Kara Shimsi has learned three lessons well - keep her head down, her fingers light, and her tithes to the syndicate paid on time.

But now a failed heist has earned her a death sentence - a one-way ticket to the toxic Waste outside the dome. Her only chance is a deal with the syndicate's most ruthless enforcer, a wolfish mountain of genetically-modified muscle named Davien.

The thought makes her body tingle with dread-or is it heat?

Mercenary Davien has one focus: do whatever is necessary to get the credits to get off this backwater mining colony and back into space. The last thing he wants is a smart-mouthed thief - even if she does have the clue he needs to hunt down whoever attacked the floating lab he and his created brothers called home.

Caring is a liability. Desire is a commodity. And love could get you killed.

https://elinwynbooks.com/star-breed/

DON'T MISS THE CONQUERED
WORLD!

He shattered her world. Can she trust him with her heart?

Giant spiders, walking trees, bloodthirsty vines.

For Jeneva, it's just another day trying to survive in the jungles of Ankau.

Until the sky ripped open, and the true monsters came through.

Now her world is under attack, and the only place of safety may be at the side of a rock-hard scaled alien.

But he's filled with secrets - how can she trust him?

Vrehx cares for nothing other than the destruction of the Xathi hordes who burned his home and killed his family.

But when a weapons test goes horribly wrong, the battle spills over to an uncharted world.

The planet is filled with lethal native life...but nothing is more dangerous than the human woman who obsesses his thoughts.

When war rages around them, can they fight together, or will his burning need for her drive them apart?

Vrehx is the first book in the science fiction romance series Conquered World. Each book is a new romance with alpha male alien warriors and women who don't put up with their nonsense. No cheating, no cliffhangers, HEA guaranteed!

Click to get Vrehx now or keep reading for a sample!
https://elinwynbooks.com/conquered-world-alien-romance/

VREHX

Streaks of plasma lit the blackness as a squadron of Valorni fighters swooped in dizzying spirals, blasting at the massive Xathi ship that filled the screens of the *Vengeance*.

We were so close it was the size of a planet. Like two steel ziggurats smashed and welded together. Not practical for space flight, but efficient enough to tear through several worlds.

Designed to intimidate.

Designed to destroy.

And we were going to stop it.

We crept closer, waiting. I sucked in my breath, geared for the inevitable.

I gritted my teeth as the bridge shook, and Karzin let out an undignified whoop from his station on the far curve of the bridge. The purple stripes on his shoulders rippled, and his excited eyes darted back and forth as if cheering on his favorite sport.

Barbarian. His crude Valorni traits got on my last nerve—not that he gave a rat's ass. Like the lot of them, he had no empathy for others. He barely listened to commands and forget anyone who didn't at least match his rank.

"You green motherfuckers aren't supposed to be hitting us, just laying cover for our approach," I snarled. "They can remember that much, can't they?"

They had only begun venturing into space when we took them into the alliance, but surely they weren't that stupid.

I hoped not.

"Fuck you," the Valorni drawled. The stretched-out

sounds of his abominable accent were like bristles to my red Skotan scales. "Not their fault we're cloaked all to hell."

What an asshole. Valorni couldn't even be bothered to speak accurately. Their drawl made it nearly impossible to understand them, and they had idiotic slang for everything.

"They were informed of our flight path before the battle." The lights of Sk'lar's implants flickered in the dim light of the bridge. "It should have been simple for them to avoid it."

I smiled just a little, glad I wasn't the only one with some common sense. Sk'lar wasn't much better than Karzin, but he was more tolerable. My biggest problem was his implants.

His artificial augmentation was just creepy and wrong. You could see them light up in biohazard green against his shiny black skin. He looked like a fucking motherboard.

The strike team leaders were chosen for their specific talents and leadership, but Sk'lar's was not stealth outside the ship.

Karzin made it a point to butt heads with all of us. That usually distracted the rest of us from being at each other's throats.

Maybe that was his intention. Whatever. He was an asshole.

Karzin shrugged off the K'ver's barely concealed criticism. "Not gonna matter in a few minutes, is it?"

The sarcasm warranted him a disapproving side-eye from Sk'lar, which he ignored. I hated to admit it, but the jackass was right. In a few minutes, we would probably all be dead.

"Gentlemen," Rouhr's quiet word from the command station silenced the chatter, "are you prepared?"

The scar that ran down the left side of his face rippled as he clenched his jaw. He was annoyed.

Of course, we were prepared.

We shut up anyway. Rouhr was very diplomatic. That's why he was in charge.

We straightened ourselves and regained our concentration.

Tension and anger clogged the air, but there was no fear. Fear had died when our families did, when our worlds had burned under the Xathi attacks.

Around the half circle, each of us activated the new weapons panels, the long seconds drawing out as they lit up and hummed. Every battle had this moment—the waiting before the storm.

But this would be different.

We owned the storm.

"Let's blow a hole in those bastards," I growled, eyes

fixed on the sickly green hull, thinking of the swarms inside.

They waited for the go ahead to surge through over the squadrons like locusts.

Nothing had been able to penetrate a Xathi hiveship before. They just plowed through and destroyed whatever they wanted, the swarms mopping up whatever the hiveship missed.

The Valorni, as annoying as they were, were inducted into the alliance for one reason. The Sugavians had worked with K'ver scientists using codialite, a mineral from the Valorni homeworld, to make one last attempt.

Just enough had been mined for this last-ditch effort —an experimental weapon that had a shot at penetrating that hull. It was rare, and we were on the losing end of this fight. We only had one shot.

We'd better make it count.

Every Skotan, K'ver, and Valorni warrior on the *Vengeance* had volunteered in the knowledge that it was a one-way trip. If this worked, the three strike teams below would board the Xathi and battle until there was nothing left.

If it didn't, we'd all die—just sooner.

Either way, the recorder satellites would beam the results of the experiment back to the scientists and engineers. We'd succeed, or they'd build a better weapon next time. That was the most important part of the mission, and we all understood how expendable we were.

The three of us locked focus on our stations as we crept closer.

"We are now in firing range, Captain," Sk'lar reported.

"Fire at will," was the only response.

Karzin sent the signal to the Valorni ships, and I started a slow count.

One.

His comrades had fought stupidly but bravely. There was no discernable pattern to the attack.

I was worried more would take friendly fire than would hit the Xathi, but they somehow made sense of the chaos, dodging fire from their comrades. If any survived the battle, they deserved to escape.

Two.

More likely the crazy bastards would follow us into the breach, but they'd earned the choice.

Three.

I activated the launch panel and braced, eyes fixed on the monitors. The adrenaline rushed through me in anticipation of the blow.

Nothing.

Not a bang or a pop or a whine. Just the hum of the

engines, and the wall of the Xathi ship growing larger on the screens.

The anticipation deflated as I looked at the panel in confusion. The damn thing was experimental, but it should at least fire. The engineers weren't brain-dead.

With a snarl, I slapped it again.

And then the universe turned inside out.

JENEVA

I was in my element.

I was where I belonged.

Completely alone in the silence, except for the gigantic bipedal tree creature with an affinity for spewing poison.

Home sweet home.

A glob of the foul stuff hissed as it ate away the earth beneath me. It was only inches from my boot, but I didn't flinch or try to move out of the way.

A rapid movement around a sorvuc was far more dangerous than its projectile poison. Its damn branches were covered in tiny neural fibers, capable of detecting incredibly small movements. The fibers were illuminated purple.

The sorvuc searched for me.

Under different circumstances, I would have found

it beautiful, but at that moment, it was just a pain in my ass.

The humidity made my short hair damp and scratchy. It clung to the curve of my neck. I longed to brush it away, but a movement like that would be a death sentence.

The luminescent purple faded away to a tranquil pink. I realized I was holding my breath.

Slowly, so slowly, I crept closer to the wide trunk of the sorvuc. I had already made an incision in its trunk. That's what pissed it off in the first place.

A necessary risk, but I only needed a few more drops of the thick scarlet fluid that seeped from the incision. The right person would pay a small fortune for its sap—or is it blood? Hell if I know.

As I slid my vial into place, ready to collect the liquid the sale of which would keep me comfortable for months, shouts erupted from somewhere nearby.

Damn it.

The sorvuc shrieked, its neural fibers flaring purple once again. It pivoted, razor-sharp leaves dangerously close to me. I rolled away, camouflaging my own movements in its rustling.

The hulking creature lumbered off in the direction the shouts came from—sort of. Its neural fibers must have picked up the sound vibrations, but with so many trees, it would have been difficult for the creature to determine the exact direction.

It's a good thing sorvuc had those fibers. They were as deaf as, well, a tree—at least, the sort of trees our ancestors brought over on their generation ship. But those trees sure as hell didn't fling poison or walk.

Walking plants were something the dense forest of Ankau had in excess. Even so, I'd take a hostile tree giant over people any day. At least they left me in peace.

Another round of shouts echoed through the trees. I clenched my teeth.

Speaking of peace.

I moved quickly and quietly through the dense forest, mindful not to disturb any of the thick vines that crisscrossed the forest floor. It was difficult to tell which ones were looking for a snack.

I spied a small herd of luurizi grazing between the roots of the docile Lenaus trees.

Their coats of lilac, sage, and pearl shimmered when they caught the mottled light bleeding through the canopy. Their silvery horns shone like jewels. It was easy to forget how deadly they were.

I was sure they could smell me.

Ordinarily, they would attack the moment they sensed an intruder. But this particular herd had become accustomed to my scent after so many years. It was an uneasy truce, but I still knew better than to take my eye off them.

Another bout of shouting brought me back to the present. It was louder this time. And stupider.

Clearly, whoever it was had a death wish, which was fine. I'd just prefer to be farther away when it happened.

The trees gave way to a small clearing. Two women, who I can only assume are the shouting morons, stood inches away from each other, their faces red with anger. They didn't notice my intrusion.

"You're not even trying anymore!" One woman, blonde and petite, hissed at the other. Her voice was tight, like she was trying to stay in control.

Sharp would have been the only way to describe her —sharp cheekbones, sharp chin, and sharp shoulders. Even her mouth was a sharp slash across her face.

I winced at her words, a headache throbbing at my temples. I almost wished something *would* come along and kill them.

"What more do you want me to do?" The other woman, dark-haired and softer than the other, answered wearily. "If I had known you were going to bring this up, I never would have agreed to meet you!"

Though they were different in coloring, they had the same nose and face shape. I guessed they were sisters—not that I cared.

"What other reason would there be to meet up?" the blonde snapped, her gray-green eyes narrowing. "What else do we have anymore?"

There was more poison in those words than there was in a fully grown sorvuc.

"I hate to interrupt," I said, startling both women.

I wanted to sound as annoyed as I felt, but my voice was brittle and raspy with disuse. I couldn't even remember the last time I had spoken aloud.

"But you really should shut up," I continued.

The blonde pivoted to face me. I was at least a head taller than her, but she somehow seemed bigger than she actually was. And the glare on her face would have made a narrisiri hesitate.

"This is none of your business," she said through clenched teeth.

"Nope, it isn't. I don't want to know about it. I don't care about it. But you really should find somewhere else to finish your screaming match," I replied.

"Do you think we're idiots? We have a howler with us," the blonde smugly fished a small black device from her pocket.

I hated those damn things. They emitted a high-pitched sound above the threshold of human hearing. It was meant to repel the creatures that stalked the forest, but I always thought it was a scam.

First of all, the people living in the cities and towns

hardly knew anything about the creatures that lived out here in the forest. Second, how would anyone know for a fact that a howler was working? No one could hear it.

"Yes, I do think you're idiots if you think that carrying a howler into the middle of aramirion territory during nesting season is a good idea," I snapped, fighting the urge to give the blonde a smug smile. "If they can hear that thing, you're screwed."

The dark-haired woman paled as she put her hand on the blonde's shoulder. The blonde stiffened at her touch.

"Leena, is that true?" the dark-haired woman whispered. Her eyes, the same color as the blonde's, nervously scanned the surrounding forest.

"How the hell would I know, Mariella? You're the one who moved all the way out to the middle of freaking nowhere!" the blonde, Leena, grumbled.

I turned to leave. Obviously, they had no intention of listening to me. Perhaps the dark-haired one, Mariella, might have seen reason, but Leena had some sort of chip on her shoulder—a chip the size of a damn ravine.

Fine. Whatever. They were adults.

I'd tried my best to warn them. It's not my fault if they chose not to listen to me.

What would I know, right? I've only been living out here for fifteen years. They would come to their senses and leave, or they would keep at it until one beast or another silenced them.

Either way, I got my forest and my silence back.

I could still feel their flurries of emotion as I marched through the undergrowth. If I was going to find another sorvuc to fill my vial, I needed to concentrate, but I couldn't do that with the feelings of two idiots in my head. I should turn back, try even harder to get them to leave.

A horrible screech unlike anything I had ever heard tore through the air. The sheer force of it drove me to my knees.

I tried to protect my ears with my hands, but it was useless. My vision blurred, stars danced behind my eyelids. I could practically feel my brain thrashing, desperate to escape that terrible sound.

Those idiots either did something to their howler, or the damn thing was malfunctioning. That had to be it.

As soon as I could get back on my feet, I staggered back to the clearing where I'd left the arguing pair. I would tear their stupid howler apart with my bare hands if I had to—anything to stop the noise.

"What the hell did you do?" I yelled.

Again, they didn't notice me when I entered the clearing, but, this time, they weren't distracted by an argument.

They stood side by side, looking up at the sky. Their faces were pale and their mouths were open in terror and confusion. I followed their gaze.

A jagged scar of pitch marred the once pristine stretch of endless blue.

The sky, *my* sky, had been torn open.

There was a beat of silence as if the whole planet had drawn in a collective breath of shock.

Then the forest erupted into chaos.

VREHX

Alarms blared around us. On the screen, all I could see were swirls of colors swallowing the Xathi.

The captain shouted orders to the rest of the crew, but his voice was distorted. It was changing—high-pitched then low and deep, fast then robotic, child-like then old, clear and loud, then soft and unintelligible.

Looking around the bridge, some of the colors were vibrant, glowing, and bright. Others were non-existent, as if all color had been drained, leaving behind various shades of gray.

Karzin's face twisted, melting down toward his midsection. I wanted to vomit, but Karzin's bird-like voice was chirping at me.

"TURN! IT! OFF!"

I turned my attention back to my control panel, just

to see it swirl around and fade. The screen was so bright, my eyes burned. The letters seemed to be dancing an old Skotan wedding march.

Looking up at the screen, the Xathi ship was ripped apart by the swirling vortex—no, it wasn't a vortex.

It was just a hole. Then it was a rip.

The only thing that stayed the same were the colors. Purple, white, and red streaks of color were covering the Xathi ship and reaching out for us.

The part of the Xathi ship already inside the rip was separating, coming apart at the seams. I could see part of the Xathi crew floating in space, then shredded by the force of the rip.

And we were getting closer to it.

I heard Rouhr's voice yelling out commands, for the engine room to go full speed ahead and drive the Xathi ship further into the rip.

It made sense. If the rip was doing this kind of damage to the "top" half, then it should destroy the rest of it as well. If we went with it, so be it.

The engines kicked in, and we were rocked forward as we crashed the *Vengeance* into the Xathi ziggurat. Our momentum pushed the Xathi ship further into the rip, and I watched as more and more of their vessels were ripped and disintegrated. It was only a few short breaths before the *Vengeance* herself began to fall through.

The energy inside her was incredible. The air carried a charge that made my scales tighten and my hair stand on end. Every color I had ever seen exploded in my eyes, bringing me a level of pain I had never felt before.

My mouth opened to scream, but no sound came out. It was as if my throat was burning and ripping in half vertically. I felt my skin and scales peel away from my body, exposing my muscles and bones to the emptiness of the void.

My eyelids, clamped as tight as I could hold them, broke apart and fell away, slowly exposing my eyes to the grayness of the void we had entered.

The bridge of the *Vengeance* was a bright gray, and everything else was varying shades of gray, getting darker and darker.

I looked at Rouhr to see his body falling apart like sand. He was yelling at us, but there was no sound.

That's when I realized that there was no sound at all. There wasn't a single solitary noise. Was the rip in space this quiet or had my ears been destroyed?

I moved my hand to touch my ear and stared in wonder at the stump at the end of my arm. I looked down, and my fingers were on my lap.

I wanted to retch. I wanted to die. I wanted to close my damn eyes.

I looked up at the screen to see the ziggurat, at least

the second half that we were attached to, reconstitute itself. It was rebuilding!

Then we were rebuilding, and the first of my senses to return was feeling. The pain was so much that I should have blacked out, except my eyelids weren't there.

When they finally returned, and I blinked for the first time, tears fell down my face. Finally, sound came back with an explosion of noise.

"...the hell is happening?"

"...are we?"

"Damage reports!"

"...off the damn switch."

"...switch, Vrehx!"

It felt as though forever was passing before my mind caught on to what they were wanting. I looked at my control panel and flipped the switch to the weapon. The void ended, and the alarms were back.

"Where the hell are we?" Rouhr asked.

"I'm not sure, Captain!" Sk'lar answered.

"Scan the—" Rouhr was interrupted as the ship shook violently, knocking most of us from our seats. "By all that is holy, what was that?"

Engineer Thribb's voice came on over the intercom. "We're losing engines, Captain. Partial power only. We've been caught by a gravitational field of some sort."

"What is generating the field?"

"I'm not sure, sir. My systems are inoperative."

"Sk'lar!"

"On it!" Sk'lar checked his system, letting out a curse that the translator didn't bother to translate. There was no need. "We're above a planet. Unfortunately, we are falling toward it."

He tried to keep his voice calm, but the slight vibrato betrayed his emotions.

The *Vengeance* wasn't built for the atmosphere of a planet. Our thrusters wouldn't work. If we fell into the atmosphere of a planet, we'd fall until we impacted with the ground, and it would be a very hard landing.

"Sir! The Xathi!" I called out, pointing at the screen.

The Xathi ziggurat was tilting, as if it were falling as well. Outside scanners adjusted and brought the full picture into view.

The planet was covered in green and blue, and above it, the Xathi ship tilted ever more as it fell.

"What planet is this, and where are the Xathi going to land?" Rouhr asked.

I brought up our positioning and the star maps in our database. "Sir, this is uncharted space for us. We don't have this planet or this system in our database."

Rouhr nodded, absorbing the information. "Crash site?"

Sk'lar turned to look at me, then at Rouhr. The look

on his face was silent resignation that something bad was going to happen.

"There appear to be seven main points of population on the planet. The Xathi are going to crash into the biggest concentration," Sk'lar said.

"Estimated survival?"

"Not good. Easily half of their city will be destroyed, killing thousands."

"And what of the Xathi? Will they survive the crash?"

"I'm not sure, sir. I'm not sure what the interior makeup of their vessel is, so I couldn't give you an accurate guess," Sk'lar replied, refusing to look at Rouhr as he stared at the computer.

"Engineer Thribb?"

"Captain?"

"Any chance of us breaking free and *not* crashing on the planet below?"

"Less than three percent, sir."

"Well, *groop*." We all looked at Rouhr in shock. "Any way to get us away from civilization?"

"Easily, as long as our engines don't finish cutting out on the way down."

"Then keep us away from any population centers. The rest of you, brace for impact!"

We watched the Xathi ziggurat crash into the center

city, the largest city, as we strapped ourselves into our seats.

The cloud of dust and flame took out half of our sensors as we entered the atmosphere. We gained speed and tilted forward, and I could feel the pressure of the straps trying to hold me up as gravity pulled me downward.

It was a struggle to breathe. The pull of gravity was forcing us downward, while the atmosphere tried to resist our penetration. I tried to lift my arm to my console to push the button for the retro rockets in order to level us out and slow us down, but I couldn't lift my arm high enough.

The ground rushed at us, and I closed my eyes.

I'll be back with you soon, my family, I thought. My only hope was that we took those bastards with us.

My head snapped forward as the *Vengeance* crashed into the ground.

There was no way that death could possibly hurt this much.

I looked to my left to see Karzin slowly and gingerly lifting his head. Just past him, S'toz's head hung forward, his chin on his chest. To my right, Sk'lar was moaning in pain, trying to reach his arm up to his head.

I slowly—oh, so, so slowly reached up to unbuckle my straps. Now free from my restraints—and oh so grateful for them, as well—I gingerly got to my feet, waiting for the blast of pain to overwhelm my senses.

"Location?" I asked.

Sk'lar answered after a short coughing fit. "We're planet-side. That's all I know. Last thing I remember seeing was that we were heading for a large forest."

That's when it finally hit me. The computers were down.

"Captain?"

A groan from behind Sk'lar answered us. Rouhr's straps had snapped, and he ended up being flung around.

"I'm still alive. Vrehx?" He pulled himself to a sitting position on the floor, his right arm dangling, blood flowing from his cheek, and his left arm clutching his ribs.

"Sir?" My left arm hurt, and it was hard to breathe, I might have cracked a rib or six. I had a headache from the depths of destruction, and I was struggling to maintain weight on my right ankle.

"Get the commanders and your teams together. Find out where we are and if we're in danger. Thribb and I will handle the ship."

I knew better than to argue with him.

I made my way to the lift, but the doors wouldn't open.

I moved three steps to my left and opened the maintenance hatch. Looking down, it was surprisingly clear.

Time to climb, I thought.

At least it was downward.

Click to get Vrehx now!

https://elinwynbooks.com/conquered-world-alien-romance/

ABOUT THE AUTHOR

I love old movies – *To Catch a Thief, Notorious, All About Eve* — and anything with Katherine Hepburn in it. Clever, elegant people doing clever, elegant things.

I'm a hopeless romantic.

And I love science fiction and the promise of space.

So it makes perfect sense to me to try to merge all of those loves into a new science fiction world, where dashing heroes and lovely ladies have adventures, get into trouble, and find their true love in the stars!

www.ingramcontent.com/pod-product-compliance
Lightning Source LLC
Chambersburg PA
CBHW070738180626
46818CB00007B/2902